Libby was about to turn away when a movement from the Griffins' house caught her eye. In the far corner of the second story, a chalky white face appeared in the window. The girl's face floated in a sea of twisted, dripping, midnight hair, and two dark eyes stared out with such intense sadness that Libby lost her breath. Hair prickled on her arms as she stared back at the girl, but Libby raised her hand in a half wave and smiled tentatively. She waited for the smile to be returned, but the girl's grave stare didn't falter. Then, the girl slowly raised a finger to the window and etched two words into the foggy glass: Help me.

POISON APPLE BOOKS

The Dead End by Mimi McCoy

This Totally Bites! by Ruth Ames

Miss Fortune by Brandi Dougherty

Now You See Me . . . by Jane B. Mason &
Sarah Hines Stephens

Midnight Howl by Clare Hutton

Her Evil Twin by Mimi McCoy

Curiosity Killed the Cat by Sierra Harimann

At First Bite by Ruth Ames

The Ghoul Next Door by Suzanne Nelson

THE GHOUL NEXT DOOR

by Suzanne Nelson

POISON APPLE

SCHOLASTIC INC.

For Colin, Aidan, and Madeline,
my loveable little ghoulies

ISBN 978-0-545-48421-3

12 11 10 9 8 7 6 5 4 3 2 1   12 13 14 15 16 17/0

Printed in the U.S.A.   40
First printing, October 2012

CHAPTER ONE

Please let him see me, Libby chanted in her head. *Let him see me just this one time.* She pressed her forehead against the classroom window and silently willed Zack's adorable head to turn. He seamlessly wove through the other players, then smoothly lobbed the ball into the goal, making Libby smile. She loved watching him play lacrosse. Now, if he would flick those aquamarine dreams in her direction, he might catch the shadow of her face in the glass. She sighed, inwardly scolding herself for trying — and failing — for the one hundredth time. It was no use. She was invisible.

She didn't exist for Zack Northam. She never had. Not back in third grade when she'd first noticed how sweet he looked sipping his chocolate milk at lunch.

And not now, four years later, at Whitford Middle School. And no wonder! Zack was the WMS prince — captain of the lacrosse team and reigning A-lister. Libby was a middling at best, camouflaged into the sea of faces Zack breezed by in the hallway every day. Libby's crush on him had always been her best-kept secret. She'd never told anyone about it, not even her best friend, Nina. What was the point? She was just like Catherine Morland in *Northanger Abbey*, her favorite novel of all time. Henry Tilney was completely out of Catherine's league, just like Zack was out of Libby's. And, unless a miracle of massive proportions occurred, he always would be.

"Miss Mason!" a sharp voice snapped, and suddenly Libby's eyes refocused and settled on the petri dish in front of her, which was erupting in flames.

"Oh!" Libby scrambled around the lab table, searching for something to dowse the fire. She dumped some water into the dish, but that only made it explode into an impressive fireworks display. She backed away from the sizzling sparks just as Mrs. Kilchek rushed over and dumped an entire box of baking soda on the mess.

Mrs. Kilchek heaved a sigh that seemed to say they'd all narrowly missed a catastrophe. "Thank goodness we didn't set off the school fire alarm," she said, then turned her piercing eyes on Libby. "Miss Mason, you cannot be safe in lab when your head is in the clouds."

Just then the bell rang, and the other students sprang from their seats, stuffing papers and books into their bags on the way out the door, giggling under their breath. Prickly heat seeped over Libby's cheeks. "I'm sorry, Mrs. Kilchek, I was just —"

Mrs. Kilchek grunted and cleared her throat, swatting at Libby's words in the air like as many annoying flies. "Never mind. Please get your things and join me at my desk."

Mrs. Kilchek marched to the front of the room while Libby threw her textbook and notepad into her bag.

"Miss Mason." Mrs. Kilchek furrowed her brow. "While you were setting fire to your lab work, I returned yesterday's tests."

"You did?" Libby asked. Oh no. She'd been too busy Zack-gazing to notice.

"Everyone's test was returned . . . except yours." Mrs. Kilchek fired somber eyes in her direction. "We need to discuss your test results."

Libby clutched her bag against her tap-dancing

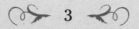

stomach, bracing herself for what came next. Whatever it was, it wouldn't be good.

Mrs. Kilchek slowly slid the test across the desk, the bloodred *D* at the top of it growing larger and larger, until it seemed to fill Libby's entire line of sight. Libby blinked hard, hoping by some small miracle the scarlet letter would disappear. It didn't.

"Another D," Mrs. Kilchek said, the line between her eyebrows deepening into a canyon. Her blunt gray hair angled toward her pointed chin, making her look even more severe (if that was possible). "That makes two so far since the start of school. And a big cause for concern."

"I'm sorry." Libby picked up the test and scanned her answers, which were smothered in red *X*'s. "I just don't understand. I studied for hours for this test, I really did." It was true. She'd been mortified by the D she'd gotten on her last test. It was the first grade she'd gotten below a B on anything in her entire life. "I'm trying to do better, but —"

"But you're struggling," Mrs. Kilchek finished for her. The canyon on her brow softened to a valley. It wasn't much, but it gave Libby the faintest glimmer of hope. "I know you're doing well in your other classes, Olivia. You're a good student, and I don't like giving bad grades to good students." She sighed. "But another grade like this on a test, and you're in danger of failing my class this semester."

"Failing!" Libby bit her lip to keep it from quivering. Failing was something that happened to other kids — kids that blew off homework and played Wii instead of studying. Failing was not an option for Libby Mason. Not now. Not ever. "But I turn in all my homework on time. I do all the lab experiments. I mean, I know my Bunsen burner set fire to Helen's backpack last week, but that was an accident! Just like today was."

Mrs. Kilchek held up her hand, and Libby stopped. "Even good students need help sometimes. I've already spoken to your parents, and we've come up with some ideas together for how to help you through this. They'll speak to you more about it after school. Keep working at it, and I'll check in with you on your progress in another week or so, okay?"

Libby opened her mouth, then shut it again, knowing there was nothing else to say. She slowly nodded, shouldering her bag. "Thank you, Mrs. Kilchek," she said softly. Mrs. Kilchek nodded, then turned away to prep for the next class.

Libby stepped out into the hallway and merged

with the crowd of kids heading toward the cafeteria. She wasn't even sure she could eat anything with her nerves playing Ping-Pong inside her, but after she chatted with Nina, she'd feel better. Nina was an expert at cheering Libby up, and had been for as long as they'd known each other.

Libby headed straight for their lunch table first, thinking Nina might be there already. Nina wasn't, but Dee and Aubrey were there, unpacking their bento boxes.

"Hey, Libby." Dee smiled from behind her tortoiseshell glasses. "I saw Mrs. Kilchek corner you after class. How bad was it?"

"Deadly," Libby said. "I'll fill you in when Nina gets here."

Dee nodded and let the topic drop, and Libby knew Dee understood that she wouldn't spill any details until Nina arrived. Libby and Nina had been inseparable since they were toddlers in the same Tot 'N' Tunes music class. They'd gone to the same schools together since preschool. They were both only children, and their parents liked to joke that they were as close to sisters as they could get without the shared DNA. They'd become friends with Dee and Aubrey last year when they all took jazz dance together. Dee and Aubrey were fun to hang out with, but Libby wasn't nearly as close to them as she was to Nina.

"Nina's buying today," Aubrey said, digging into her pasta salad. "She'll be back in a sec."

Libby glanced over to the lunch line, and her heart, which was having a rough day, hit the floor. Sure enough, there was Nina, her strawberry-blond hair piled in a shabby chic knot on top of her head, her lunch tray balanced effortlessly on her hip. And she was smiling brightly and chatting away easily with . . . Zack Northam!

Libby's glance turned into a full-blown stare. Zack had never spoken to Nina before, at least, not that Libby knew. But Zack was doing more than speaking now. He was flashing his brilliant smile at Nina, and laughing like she was the most entertaining girl in the room.

Libby dropped down onto the lunch bench next to Dee, shell-shocked. Why had Zack suddenly noticed Nina, today of all days? But as Libby watched the two of them, she knew why. Because over the summer, Nina had undergone an extreme makeover of the Italian variety. She'd gone to Florence with her parents, and in the three months she was gone, Nina had gotten taller, prettier, and even a little curvier. And that wasn't all that had changed about her. She'd ditched the glasses she wore every day for contact lenses to show off her bright green eyes, and she'd adopted a whole new bohemichic wardrobe, too. Today Nina was looking übercute in a pink leather skirt and black top, filigree dangly earrings, and a shimmery burgundy belted scarf. It was no wonder Zack had noticed her. Nina had left the pumpkin patch behind and was ready for the palace.

Nina said good-bye to Zack and headed toward their table, her cheeks blushing a pretty shade of pink along the way. Libby quickly pretended to focus on her lunch so Nina wouldn't know she'd been staring.

"Ciao, bella!" Nina said, giving Libby a friendly hip-bump to get her to slide down the bench to make room. "Wow, I think Italy may have spoiled my taste buds forever. Where's Napoli when you need it? This pizza dough looks like cardboard." She took a bite, then grimaced dramatically. "Tastes like it, too."

"But the wait in line must have been worth it," Libby said, elbowing Nina playfully and waiting to see what Nina's reaction would be.

"What?" Nina blanked, then the rosiness swept over her face again, and she smiled. "Oh, you mean

Zack?" She shrugged. "He had some questions about the English essay due in Mr. Gossett's class next week. That's all."

"Oh, right," Libby said with a nod. "I forgot you have English with him."

"Lucky." Aubrey grinned.

Nina giggled. "Do you know what's hysterical? Zack introduced himself to me today, and asked me when I moved here. He didn't recognize me at all, and I've been in school with him for years. Maybe it's my new contacts."

"I think it's *definitely* your Mediterranean tan," Libby teased, trying hard to push her own feelings away. Nina was downplaying the whole thing, but Libby could tell that she was thrilled that Zack had noticed her. And Libby couldn't blame her. After all, what girl wouldn't be happy to have Zack's attention? Libby couldn't even allow herself to get irritated with Nina. That wouldn't be fair. After all, Nina didn't know about Libby's crush on Zack, so he wasn't off limits. But as Libby tried her best to pretend she didn't care, her muscles tensed uncomfortably.

"I can't believe you scored a class with Zack this year," Dee said to Nina with a combination of envy and admiration. "Better you than me. If I had English with Zack, I'd be failing. I would never be able to focus on Shakespeare with him around."

At the mention of failing, Libby's stomach turned sour, and she dropped her barely eaten sandwich back into her bento box. Almost immediately, Nina's hand was on her shoulder. That was one of the things Libby loved the most about Nina. She had this way of picking up on Libby's moods without Libby even having to say anything. It was so nice to have someone know her that well.

"What's wrong?" Nina asked. "You're completely whiting out on us."

Libby took a deep breath, then told Nina and the girls about her science test and her talk with Mrs. Kilchek.

"Oh, Libby," Nina said, hugging her. "I'm so sorry. That is a serious stressor." Then a smile snuck across her face, and she giggled. "But I would've loved to see Mrs. Kilchek's face when your experiment got flambéed."

"Think Grim Reaper. And it was *not* funny." Although even she couldn't help a small giggle at the memory. But then the seriousness of the situation hit her all over again, and she groaned and dropped her head into her hands. "My parents are going to kill me. They'll lock me in my room and feed me through the keyhole. You won't see me again until I'm a stooped old hag."

Nina rolled her eyes. "Whoa. Which one of your goth novels did you pull that from?"

"*The Watcher in the Attic*," Libby admitted sheepishly. "I just finished it last night. It was incredible. Elle is imprisoned by her awful uncle for twenty years, but when she finally breaks free, her true love is still waiting for her." She pulled the book out of her bag, where it had been nestled with the two other novels she'd just checked out from the library. "Do you want to borrow it?"

Nina laughed. "Um, you keep offering, and I keep saying no. You know that moldy castles and hidden corpses aren't my thing." She glanced at the cover of the book, a picture of a horror-stricken girl running from a cloaked villain, and her face wrinkled in distaste. "If you loved reading about photosynthesis and osmosis as much as those gothic romances, you'd be golden."

"And completely brain-dead," Libby said, shuddering at the thought of giving up her reading.

"Well, at least you don't have to break the news about your grade to the parental units yourself,"

Nina said, offering up the bright side of the situation, just like she always did. "Mrs. Kilchek's already done that for you."

"Yup, no doubt giving my parents more time to think up a torturous punishment." Libby sighed. "I can't go home. I can't deal. . . ." She thought for a minute, then grabbed Nina's arm hopefully. "Unless you come home with me? Maybe if you're there you can help me talk to them, and they'll take pity on my poor, science-challenged soul."

Nina laughed. "It won't be that bad. You just have to face them."

"But you're so much better at these things than I am," Libby said, and she knew it was true. Nina had always been the brave one — the one who'd confessed proudly to painting the kitchen floor with finger paints when they were five. The one who'd convinced Libby to go waterskiing for the first time, and horseback riding, and to try jazz dance. "Please, come with me."

Nina smiled, but then a trace of embarrassment crossed her face. "I would come over if I could, but I can't today." She hesitated, clearly struggling with what was coming next. "Um, I'm going to the mall with Alia Dawson after school."

Libby froze, her jaw dropping, and she noticed that even Dee and Aubrey had stopped eating to stare at Nina in disbelief.

"Alia?" Libby repeated, and she suddenly wondered if she'd stepped into a parallel universe. Because if Zack Northam was the prince of WMS, then Alia was the reigning queen. She was the most popular girl in school, and she and her group of Primas (short for *Prima Donnas*) never talked to middlings like Libby and Nina. *Ever.* At least until today. "But she's a Prima," Libby stammered. "She doesn't even know any of us exist."

"Well, she does now." Nina's smile bristled ever so slightly, and Libby felt a stab of guilt for being so blunt. "She stopped me in the hallway yesterday," Nina said shyly. "She loved the tunic dress I had on. I told her I got it in Florence. But then she asked me to go shopping with her to help her pick out some new clothes. She said she likes my style."

"Wow," Dee said, admiration ringing in her voice. "Alia coveting your clothes. That's history in the making right there."

Nina shrugged. "It's really no biggie. She'll find out soon enough that I can't afford any of the designers she wears, anyway. I'm sure she'll be bored with me after an hour." She glanced at Libby. "I really am sorry I can't be with you this afternoon for the attack of the parentals. But . . ." she added hurriedly, "you know you could come with me to the mall, if you want."

"Thanks for the invite," Libby said, but she couldn't read Nina's expression. Was she being sincere, or just polite? "I can't go, anyway, not with the D hanging over my head. I'd be in even bigger trouble if I went to the mall instead of home to face Mom and Dad."

"Okay," Nina said just as the bell rang and throngs of kids began filing out of the cafeteria to fifth period. She stood, then offered up an encouraging smile. "I'm sure it'll be okay. Call me after it's over, if you can."

"I will," Libby said. She waved good-bye to Dee and Aubrey, then trudged to her history class with sinking spirits. In the last two hours, her GPA had nosedived and her best friend had suddenly become a magnet for the popular kids at school. After the morning she'd had, maybe facing her parents wouldn't be so bad after all.

CHAPTER TWO

She was wrong. When Libby stepped off the school bus that afternoon, she knew beyond a doubt that facing her parents wouldn't be bad . . . it would be absolutely unbearable. Both her mom *and* her dad were waiting for her at the top of their driveway with their arms folded and their foreheads wrinkled in concern. Even their eyes were frowning. It was three in the afternoon, so her dad had come home from work early, which he only did in emergencies. Libby took a deep breath, wondering briefly if there was any chance of escape. The deep rumbling of an engine made her glance next door for a moment, and she saw a massive moving van pulling into the gravel driveway. The house next door had been vacant for over six months, but it looked like there would finally be someone moving in. Too bad Libby couldn't move in with them . . . right now.

She walked toward her parents, her feet fighting her the whole way.

"So," she said hesitantly, "I'm hoping you're out here to welcome the new neighbors?"

"Try again," her dad said darkly.

Libby's shoulders slumped. "Do you think they'd be willing to adopt a daughter if her parents disown her?"

Her mom couldn't manage a smile, but the corners of her eyes lifted just a bit. "I doubt you'll be disowned today. But we'll see." She put an arm around Libby. "Come on inside, and we'll figure this mess out."

Luckily, Libby didn't have to explain much about her science grade. As it turned out, Mrs. Kilchek had given her parents a very thorough description of the situation. But unfortunately, that didn't mean Libby was off the hook. Not even close.

"We know you're trying," her dad said to her. "We don't doubt you're studying. But it's just not clicking for you." He exchanged a *parents-unite* glance with her mom. Libby hated that glance.

Her mom took over from there. "Mrs. Kilchek told us your next test is in two weeks. So, until then, you're going to focus on studying even more. We're taking away some of your privileges until you can get your grade up." She looked soberly at Libby. "That means no hanging out with Nina after school, no trips to the mall or the movies. You're to come straight home every day."

"But, Mom!" Libby started. She could not be apart from Nina for two whole weeks. "You're giving my social life the death penalty. Come on!"

"Olivia, we're not finished," her dad said firmly, then sighed. "We wish you had told us about that first D yourself right after it happened."

"I'm sorry," Libby said. "I didn't think I'd get another bad grade. I really didn't. I thought I could turn things around."

"If you'd told us," her mom said, "we could've gotten you help sooner."

Libby looked up from where she'd been boring a hole in the table with her eyes. Oh no. She did not like the sound of this. "Help?"

Her mom nodded. "I called Adam Briggs's mother this afternoon. He's coming over to tutor you in the afternoons three times a week."

Libby's jaw nearly hit the floor. "Adam Briggs! He can't be my tutor. He spends lunch every day with the science club conducting experiments. He talks like a computer program. He's a complete —"

"Genius," her mom finished for her.

Libby dropped her head onto the table, groaning. *Genius* was not the word she'd been looking for, even if it was true. Adam lived a few blocks over from her, but she'd never actually gotten to know him too well. That was because his nose was constantly buried in some college-level science textbook. He'd won every district science fair since kindergarten, and when he was ten, he'd achieved a weird sort of fame in Whitford for becoming the youngest kid ever to win the state science fair. He didn't even take science classes at their middle school, for goodness' sake. His mom drove him over to the high school twice a week so that he could take AP biology and chemistry there. There was no doubt about it. Anyone who was that good at science had to be some kind of freak of nature, and now he was going to be tutoring her! It was too much. She'd die a slow and painful death by beaker.

"Adam will be a wonderful tutor, I'm sure," her mom said, ignoring Libby's horror. "And we don't expect you to study all the time. I thought a little hands-on experience would be helpful, too. So when you're not studying, you can help out our new neighbors, Mr. and Mrs. Griffin, with their garden."

"Are you kidding me?" Libby shrieked, pushing her chair back from the table. That was it. The last straw. "I'm under house arrest and I have to do yard work, too?" Angry heat flashed across her face. "I'm being punished for something I couldn't even help!"

"No," her dad said, "this is not punishment. But if you don't get at least a B on your next test, you won't be allowed to attend the school Harvest Festival either. And I'm afraid that *will* be a punishment. We don't want to see that happen."

Libby stared at them in disbelief. "But I'm on the decorating committee for the Harvest Festival!" she cried. "It's the biggest school event this fall." And that wasn't even an exaggeration. Kids had been talking about it since the first day of school, and Nina had immediately jumped on the bandwagon. She'd volunteered to be the president of the decorating committee and had immediately strong-armed Libby (and Aubrey and Dee) into joining, too. But how could Libby be on the decorating committee for the Harvest Festival and then be a no-show on the big night? If that didn't kill her social life for her entire middle-grade career, she didn't know what would.

"You can still be on the committee as long as it meets during school hours," her mom said. "And, as long as you pull your grade up, you will be able to go to the festival. We just want you to focus on understanding science and improving your grade without any distractions. That's all."

"That's all?" Libby could hear her voice getting louder and louder. "You've taken away everything!"

"This is the way it's going to be," her dad said, and Libby knew there was nothing she could say that would change a thing. Her dad's face was set in stone, and the discussion was over.

She grabbed her bag and blew past her parents, wanting to get to her room before tears came. She made sure to slam her bedroom door especially loud for full effect, then threw herself onto the cushioned seat in her bay window.

She quickly dialed Nina's number on her cell phone. When Nina picked up, there was a crackle of static, followed by the loud buzz of music and voices in the background.

"Libby?" Nina's voice was muffled and distant. "Is that you?"

"You are not going to *believe* what my parents are doing to me," Libby started. "I'm condemned."

"You're what?" Nina asked. "Libby, I can barely hear you. I'm at the mall right now with Alia and —"

"Oh yeah," Libby said. "I totally forgot. You should go, and we can talk more later. Have fun."

Nina hesitated on the other end of the line. "Are you sure? I really do want to hear what happened. You sound upset. It's just not a good time right now."

"No, it's fine." Libby heard a muffled giggle in the background, and imagined Alia laughing over some ugly generic-brand shirt she'd just pulled off a clothes rack. Nina was probably having a terrific time with her. That thought made a sudden loneliness settle over Libby. "Can I call you tonight?"

"Um, you can try," Nina said. "I'm just not sure when I'll be home. If I don't pick up, you can fill me in on everything tomorrow at school, okay?"

"Sure. No problem. Bye." Libby tossed her cell phone down, and flopped back onto her pillows. So this was it. How pathetic. While her best friend was at the mall having fun, her own world had suddenly shrunk down to the size of her bedroom. Her life was officially over.

She stared glumly out the window, watching the movers shuffling boxes into and out of the slate gray colonial next door. The house was nestled among birch and maple trees, which were slowly dropping their waterlogged leaves in scattered patches along the wide stretch of lawn and shrubs. It looked much like the other houses in the neighborhood, but the fact that it had been vacant for so long gave it a stark, dreary mood the others didn't have. Libby had never liked that house.

A steady rain had started falling, and a woman with gray-streaked brown hair stood in the driveway under a black umbrella, overseeing the movers. *She must be Mrs. Griffin,* Libby thought. She looked like she was about the same age as Libby's mom, but Mrs. Griffin's eyes and mouth — her whole body — drooped with tiredness. Or maybe sadness? Libby wasn't sure, but the woman did not look like she smiled much, if ever.

Libby was about to turn away when a movement from the Griffins' house caught her eye. In the far corner of the second story, a chalky white face appeared in the window. The girl's face floated in a sea of twisted, dripping, midnight hair, and two dark eyes stared out with such intense sadness that Libby lost her breath. Hair prickled on her arms as she stared back at the girl, but Libby raised her hand in a half wave and smiled tentatively. She waited for the smile to be returned, but the girl's grave stare didn't falter. Then, the girl slowly raised a finger to the window and etched two words into the foggy glass: HELP ME.

Iced lightning flashed through Libby's veins. *Help me*? Was it a joke, as in, *Save me from this boring town?* Maybe. But this girl didn't look much like the joking type. In fact, there was something downright creepy about her sunken eyes and ashen face. Suddenly, Libby sensed someone else watching her, and she glanced at the driveway to find Mrs. Griffin's eyes burning into her. Then, Mrs. Griffin turned toward the second-story window. Libby looked back at it, too, but the girl had vanished. Even the words *Help me* had already streaked into illegibility on the windowpane.

Libby shuddered, then ducked out of her window seat before Mrs. Griffin could start with the evil eye again. Well, if the new neighbors were friendly, they had a strange way of showing it. And Libby was going to have to work for Mrs. Griffin? What a treat that would be. There was no doubt about it. It was going to be a long and painful two weeks.

That night, after trying (and failing) to decode the latest chapter in her science book, Libby crawled into bed, defeated and empty. She tried to call Nina, but all she got was her voice mail. Of course she was still out with Alia. Nina was busy having a life, unlike her. Thoroughly grumpy now, she tried to close her eyes, but sleep wouldn't come. A face hovered behind her eyelids — the face of the girl in the window. Libby pulled her covers over her head to ward off those penetrating eyes that, even now, seemed to be watching her from the shadows.

CHAPTER THREE

Libby craned her neck around her locker and scanned the faces in the hallway one more time. But it was pointless. The lunch bell had rung, and there was still no sign of her.

"And who might you be searching for?" Nina said, slipping from the stampede of students to come stand by Libby. "Looking for a new crush in the hallways?"

"Ha." Libby slammed her locker shut, and they began working their way toward the cafeteria. "You know all my crushes are made of ink and paper," she lied.

"Hey, someday you'll fall for a *non*-fiction guy," Nina said. "I'm holding out hope."

"Not happening." Libby grinned. "I was actually looking for the girl that moved in next door to me."

"You mean from the new family you're doing manual labor for?" Nina joked.

"Yup." Libby nodded. Before first period that morning, Libby had filled Nina in on the mandatory gardening detail her parents had inflicted on her along with her two-week house arrest. She'd been worried about how Nina would act after hanging out with Alia yesterday afternoon. But to Libby's relief, Nina was the same as always. She'd barely even mentioned Alia or her trip to the mall, and she'd been genuinely upset to hear about Libby's situation at home.

"The Griffin girl looks like she's our age," Libby said now. "I thought she might be starting school today. But I haven't seen her at all."

"Well, we only have one middle school in this town. If she's enrolled, this is where she'd come. Maybe she stayed home an extra day to unpack." Nina shrugged. "Is she nice?"

"I haven't even really talked to her yet," Libby said as they got in the lunch line. "I just saw her from the window. She was pretty pale. I thought she might be sick or something. But I was going to try to introduce myself today." What she didn't tell Nina was that she'd really been hoping to find out what the "help me" weirdness had been all about yesterday, too. It still gave her shivers, thinking about it. "Oh, well, maybe I'll see her this afternoon. I have to go help Mrs. Griffin with her yard after my first torture session with Adam, the walking, talking textbook."

"I'm sorry." Nina squeezed Libby's arm. "But he might not be so bad. Maybe there's some closet coolness in there somewhere." She offered an encouraging smile. "Make it your mission to find it and save him from his nerdy ways."

Libby giggled. "I'll try to remember that."

"Good." Nina checked her watch. "Hey, we need to eat quick before our first decorating-committee meeting."

Libby sighed. "Do I really have to go with you? It seems kind of pointless now. I probably won't even be *at* the festival."

"Watch your mouth, young lady," Nina snapped in no-nonsense fashion. "Pessimism never did anyone any favors. Statements of affirmation. That's what you need." She inhaled and closed her eyes, like she was meditating. "Repeat after me. I *will* pass science. I *will* go to the festival."

"I *will* be bored out of my mind in this meeting," Libby said, then wailed when Nina slugged her arm.

"It is such a good thing you have me around," Nina said. "Otherwise, you'd never do anything. You'd hole up in your bedroom reading your books and never see daylight." She smiled at Libby and plopped a turkey sandwich onto her tray. "Here, Madame Librarian. If you're going to die of boredom, you might as well do it on a full stomach."

It was twenty minutes later, and Libby hadn't died of boredom yet. But she was close. She stifled a yawn and stretched her legs across the gym bleachers. Nina had started off the meeting, explaining that the Harvest Festival would involve a Ferris wheel and a haunted hayride, and finally, a dance, all to be held on the school grounds. Aubrey was writing down detailed minutes of the whole meeting, but so far, not much of anything had happened. There were about a dozen other kids in attendance, and none of them seemed very willing to offer up opinions or ideas.

"So," Nina was saying now, "the themes that have been done in the past were Harry Potter, Pirates of the Caribbean, and a Thriller theme. Principal Stelson wants something fresh this year. She said she'd rather not do something from pop culture again." She smiled expectantly at the other kids. "Okay, then, let's brainstorm!"

Libby stared at her jeans, pretending to be intensely interested in the gold stitching at their seams. Speaking in front of groups larger than, say, one person was not her strong suit, and she wasn't about to start now. Let the other kids brainstorm and come up with the theme. She'd be happy to decorate with any theme once it was decided on.

But an uneasy minute passed in silence, and Libby could virtually hear Nina in her head, saying, *Libby! Help me out here!* Then Nina did it for real.

She cleared her throat, smiled encouragingly, and said, "Libby. I'm sure you have some ideas. Can you *please* share?" She was still smiling, but Libby was sure Nina had her teeth clenched behind those lips.

Libby cringed as her hands and neck turned clammy. Why did Nina always do this to her? Okay, okay, a theme. She could do this. She could —

"Northanger Abbey," she blurted, a little too loudly.

"What?" Nina said, tilting her head to ask for clarification.

"You know," Libby said. "The Jane Austen book, *Northanger Abbey*. The setting is this dreary old castle. It's very gothic, and the heroine is convinced there is some kind of dark mystery surrounding it."

The other kids blinked at her blankly, and it was clear she was quickly losing her audience. "We could decorate the gym like the inside of a castle," she said. "You know, stone walls, maybe some candelabras or chandeliers." She was throwing out whatever popped into her head. "We could even make some Victorian-style caskets."

"Yeah!" Dee joined in, trying to help out. "That could be cool. We could have a skeleton playing a piano or organ, and bats hanging from the ceiling."

Slowly, the other kids were starting to come to life, nodding and smiling, and throwing in their own suggestions. And Nina grinned with a mixture of excitement and relief.

"Okay, people, this could be it," she said. "Let's take a quick vote before the bell. All in favor of the gothic castle theme, raise hands."

A dozen hands shot into the air just as the bell rang.

"Great!" Nina called as everyone headed for the gym exits. "See you all next week. I'll split you into two groups of shifts to work on decorations. Look for the lists to get posted on the school bulletin board. Thank you!"

Libby was about to tackle Nina, but Nina had slyly grabbed her things and was scooting out the door.

"Gotta run!" she sing-songed. "Don't want to be late to class!"

And with that, she was gone, and Libby had to wait three more periods before catching up with her at her locker after school. But Libby wasn't about to let Nina forget.

"I can't believe you did that to me at lunch," she hissed. "You completely spotlighted me out of nowhere. I should never have let you talk me into being on that committee."

Nina rolled her eyes. "You're still stuck on the committee meeting? Yeesh."

"You know I hate talking in front of people." Libby shoved her books into her bag and followed Nina along the hallway toward the school doors.

Nina blinked wide eyes, all innocence. "Well, what was I supposed to do? No one was saying *anything*. It was a total stalemate. And I knew you'd have a good idea, and you did." Nina gave an impish grin. "Libby, you never realize how much you have to offer. You can't spend your life as wallpaper. Sometimes you just need a little push, that's all. And *that's* why you have me." She leaned her head on Libby's shoulder. "You can't stay mad at me, anyway. You know you love me."

Libby tried to keep the frown on her face, but it was tough. Nina always managed to make it seem ridiculous that she was mad at all. "It *was* a good idea. . . ." Libby finally conceded, reluctantly.

"A great one!" Nina said, hugging Libby. They stepped out into the chilly afternoon sunshine. The yellow buses had already pulled up at the curb, and they walked over to get in the bus line. "Now I just have to figure out our budget with Principal Stelson and then we can start shopping for decorations."

Libby's spirits sank. Picking out the decorations had been one of the things about being on the committee that she'd actually looked forward to. And she was going to miss it. "You mean *you* can start shopping," she said. "You'll have to go without me."

"Oh, shoot, that's right." Nina's face wilted. "This stinks. No after-school girl bonding for two weeks. I'm going to miss you so much!"

"Me too," Libby said, happy to hear Nina say it out loud. It was nice to know that even with invites from Alia, Nina still wanted to spend time with her, too. "Promise not to have too much fun without me, okay?"

"Of course not," Nina vowed solemnly. "And I'll make sure I pick out some fab decorations. Ones with a real gothic flair, just for you. Deal?"

"Deal." Libby smiled, but her smile instantly froze with shyness when — OMG! — Zack walked over to them.

"Hey, Nina," he said, giving Nina an adorable grin. He nodded absently but politely toward Libby. "Thanks for lending me your notes. I think they'll really help me make sense of all the 'thee' and 'thou' stuff. I'll give them back to you tomorrow."

"No problem," Nina said easily, tilting her head at the perfect angle to make her hair catch the sunlight. "Take your time."

"Okay," he said. "See you tomorrow." Then he climbed onto his bus.

Libby's heart hammered noisily in her chest, and

she'd suddenly forgotten how to speak. But next to her, Nina was beaming and blushing prettily.

"See you tomorrow. Text me if you need any more help!" Nina called after him.

Libby waited until the bus doors closed, and then she blurted, "Text me?!?" She gawked at Nina. "He's texting you now?"

Nina tucked her broad smile into her coat. "Well, I'm helping him with English. He's having trouble with Shakespeare, and he asked me to proofread his essays for him. He's a horrible speller." Her eyes followed Zack's bus as it drove away. "But . . . he's nice. I like talking to him."

"That's good," Libby said stiffly as a knot formed in the pit of her stomach. Suddenly, she had an illogical urge to wipe Nina's smile off her face. And before she could stop herself, she added, "I wouldn't get too used to talking to him though."

Nina's smile faltered. "What do you mean?"

Libby shrugged. "I don't know. It's just that he usually hangs around with Alia and the Primas."

"The Primas," Nina repeated, then frowned. "I don't think you should call them that anymore. You don't know them, and they're not all like that."

Libby flushed. There had been a time when Nina had laughed at that nickname right alongside Libby. And now she was criticizing Libby for ever having used it in the first place? "Okay," she muttered. "It's just a joke between us. You never seemed to care before."

"Well, maybe I do now," Nina said quietly. "And so what if Zack usually hangs around with them? That doesn't mean he can't speak to me if he wants to."

"No, I know that." Libby shrugged. "I just hope he's not using you to boost his English grade. It seems kind of strange that he's paying so much attention to you out of nowhere. That's all." It wasn't a nice thing to say, and Libby knew it, even if it was partially true. But she couldn't help herself. Zack Northam had finally been within five feet of her, and she'd acted like a tongue-tied idiot, while Nina had breezed through beautifully.

"Strange?" Nina repeated, doubt edging into her voice. "You really think so?" The sparkle in her eyes dimmed a bit, but she didn't wait for Libby to respond. She shook her head, straightened her shoulders, and refreshed her smile. "Well, I better get on my bus before it leaves without me." She hugged Libby. "Promise to call me later once you escape the torture chamber?"

"Promise," Libby said. She waved to Nina, then ran to her own bus. She found a seat, then pulled out a new novel, *The Door Beneath the Stairs*. If she was going to have to suffer through an hour of science, she owed herself fifteen minutes of fun first.

Fifteen minutes of fun was all she got, because the second she walked into the kitchen, she found Adam seated at the table, a science textbook (*groan*) and a laminated miniature version of the periodic table (*double groan*) spread out in front of him. Her mom waved her into the room as she put some chips and salsa on the table.

"Here are some snacks for you two," she said. "I'll leave you alone so you can get started." She gave Libby a *you-can-do-it* smile, and scurried out of the room while Libby's cheeks caught fire.

"Hi, Libby," Adam said cheerfully as he tried to smooth down his brown curls, which were sprouting hopelessly from his head in all directions. He smiled, revealing gleaming white teeth, and Libby realized the last time she'd seen him he'd still had his braces. He'd gotten a lot taller over the summer, too.

"Hey," Libby said dully.

A few moments of awkward silence followed, then Adam said, "So . . . what do you do with two dead D's?"

Libby stared at him. He couldn't possibly be making a joke? "Um . . ."

"You barium!" He barked a short laugh, then cleared his throat. He scribbled the word on his notepad and swiveled it in her direction. "Barium? Get it? It's the fifth element . . . a metal . . ." His voice died away while his cheeks flushed crimson.

Libby suddenly realized her mouth had fallen open, and she quickly shut it. "I got it the first time," she said. "I just can't believe you actually said it out loud."

"Me either," Adam blurted. He rubbed the back of his hand across his eyebrows, as if he were trying to erase the joke from his mind. "That was terrible."

"It was," Libby said, not even bothering to tone down the brutal honesty. She wasn't usually so blunt, but she didn't really care what Adam thought of her. So she didn't have anything to lose. "Does anyone actually find that funny?"

Adam sighed. "Not really, no. You can chalk it up to complete social ineptness. It's a bad trait of mine."

Well, that surprised her. Apparently, he wasn't afraid of being honest either.

Suddenly, their eyes met, and they both burst out laughing.

"I just didn't know what to say," Adam managed to get out between gulps of laughter, "and you looked really ticked off when you walked in."

Libby laughed harder this time, until her eyes blurred, and all at once, the wall she'd promised to keep up came crashing down. "I was mad," she admitted, sitting down across from him. "I know I sounded totally witchy just now. That's not me at all. But . . . I really hate this."

"Science or tutoring?" Adam asked.

"Both." Then she slapped her hand over her mouth. "Sorry. No offense."

Adam shrugged. "I'm a seventh grader who has to survive two classes a week in the presence of a bunch of high school seniors. I have thick skin. And I know science isn't everybody's thing."

"No kidding," Libby said.

"So, let's make a deal," Adam said. "You give me a fair shot. I won't tell any more awful jokes."

"Sounds fair," Libby said after thinking it over. "But don't expect too much of me. Mrs. Kilchek has started putting the fire extinguisher next to me before lab starts. That's how bad I am."

Adam snorted. "That's not so awful. My mom keeps the fire department on speed dial. Last year, I conducted an experiment involving Christmas ornaments and our microwave oven. You should have seen the fireballs that shot out when my mom opened the microwave door. She *still* hasn't recovered."

Libby giggled. "That makes me feel better."

Adam opened the science textbook to the chapter they were on. "So, what's the worst part of it for you?"

"That." Libby pointed to the periodic table. "It's like hieroglyphics."

"Okay." Adam nodded. "So we'll start with that. Your mom says you like to read. Tell me about some of your favorite books and characters."

Libby smirked. "How is that going to help me with the periodic table?"

"We're going to make each element into one of your characters." He slid the periodic table over so it was sitting in between them. "You're just going to have to trust me."

Libby hesitated. There was no way this could possibly work, but she'd promised she'd give him a fair shot, so here went nothing. "Okay," she said, and started talking.

By the time her mom popped her head into the kitchen to say the hour was up, Libby was actually filling in a blank periodic table from memory. She wasn't doing that badly either. She didn't know all the elements yet, but Adam's method of giving the elements characteristics of some of her favorite heroes and heroines seemed to be working, amazingly enough.

"Tomorrow, we'll tackle ions," Adam said as he stood up to go.

Libby moaned. "I'm not going to make it."

Adam leaned in toward her conspiratorially. "There's chocolate involved."

"Really?" Libby laughed. "I'm in."

She watched him bike away, then shut the door, ready to escape to her bedroom for a nap to recoup her maxed-out brain.

"Not so fast," her mom called when Libby's foot hit the first stair. "You have a date with Mrs. Griffin's garden, remember?"

Libby whimpered. "No naps allowed in the house of pain, huh?"

"Not today, sweetie. Have fun!" her mom said in the most annoyingly cheerful way imaginable.

Libby changed into her grungy sweats, pulled on her oldest pair of sneakers, and forced herself to head outside, clinging to the hope that maybe it would start pouring and Mrs. Griffin would be a no-show.

As luck would have it, there wasn't a cloud in the sky, and Mrs. Griffin was already in her front yard, an extra pair of gardening gloves in her hand.

"Hello, Olivia," she said quickly. "I thought you could help me with some mulching today."

"Okay," Libby said, then she glanced toward the house, wondering if the Griffin girl would come out to join them. It made sense that if Libby was going to be doing the yard work, their own daughter would be, too. But there was no sign of her.

Mrs. Griffin pointed to two wheelbarrows, one filled with loose chips and one filled with . . . Libby's nose knew the answer before Mrs. Griffin said it.

"The manure fertilizer goes on first, and then the wood chips," Mrs. Griffin said.

"Okay," Libby managed to choke out, trying not to breathe too deeply.

Mrs. Griffin examined Libby's face for a few seconds, and Libby had the strange sense that Mrs. Griffin was waiting to see if Libby would complain. But Libby kept quiet, and Mrs. Griffin abruptly handed Libby the gloves and a shovel. "You can start with the azaleas and then work your way around the front." She turned toward the house, then stopped. "If you need me, please ring the doorbell."

"Thank you," Libby called, but Mrs. Griffin was already shutting the front door. Libby stared after her. Mrs. Griffin hadn't smiled even one time. Wow. And had she imagined it, or did Mrs. Griffin seem almost angry with her? Libby had no clue what the reason for that would be, but Mrs. Griffin had definitely been on edge.

And an hour later, with the fine manure dusting her clothes and hair, Libby definitely felt like her job was a kind of awful punishment. Even in the brisk air, she was sweating. The stink of the fertilizer filled her nose, and she was sure that by now her clothes reeked, too. Well, at least no one she knew was here to see her in this shape, or she might never be able to show herself at school again.

But just as she thought it, she sensed that someone, something, *was* watching her. Libby shivered, a chill slinking up her spine. She turned around and there, under the shadows of a weeping willow a few feet away from her, was the girl. She was even paler now than Libby remembered, with gray circles under her charred brown eyes. Her hair was a tangled mess again, rivulets of water running from it like she'd just stepped out of the shower. Libby thought the poor girl must be freezing without a coat on. The temp couldn't have been much higher than fifty today. That was when she noticed it. The water wasn't just dripping from her hair, but from her jeans and shirt, too. The girl was soaking wet all over, but she wasn't even shivering. Bizarre. Clearly, this girl had some issues.

"Hi," Libby said, determined to be polite despite the strangeness of it all. "I'm Libby, your friendly neighborhood child laborer."

The girl didn't move. Her eyes stayed locked on Libby, unblinking.

Libby cleared her throat. Well, this was awkward. "Um, did you come to help out?" she tried again.

"That would be so great. And I could definitely use a hand, if you're not busy."

The girl opened her mouth, and finally two words, half whispered, half moaned, slipped out: "I can't."

The way she said it — the hoarse way she gurgled the words — made Libby involuntarily shudder. Something was wrong with her. Maybe she was sick. Or really shy? Libby hoped there was a reason, because if not, then this girl was just downright creepy.

"Well, okay then. No problem," Libby said, searching for a way to end this uncomfortable conversation. "Maybe I'll see you at school tomorrow?"

The girl glanced back at the house, her eyes widening in fear. "I have to go," she whispered, her voice strained in panic now. "I'm . . . not allowed to leave for very long." With that, she ran out from under the tree and around the side of the house, disappearing.

"Wait!" Libby called, standing up to start after her. "What's your name?"

She was gone, but then her name echoed back, riding on the low moan of the chilly wind, hollow and unearthly: "Julia."

Libby stared after her, realizing for the first time that her heart was pounding wildly. She had to stifle a scream a second later when frosty fingers brushed her shoulder. She jumped up and nearly slammed into Mrs. Griffin, who was standing over her, frowning.

"That's fine for today," Mrs. Griffin said briskly, surveying her shrubbery with a keen eye. It must have passed inspection because she handed Libby a ten-dollar bill and walked away across the lawn. Then she paused. "Libby, I heard your voice out here earlier. I'd appreciate it if you'd chat on your cell phone some other time. I'm sure your friends can wait."

Libby flushed. "But I wasn't on my cell," she blurted. "I was talking to your —"

But the front door shut with a definitive *click,* and Mrs. Griffin was gone. Libby sat stunned on the grass, the cold, damp earth seeping through the knees of her sweats. What was that all about? Mrs. Griffin must have heard her talking to Julia, but then hadn't she heard Julia's voice, too? And she hadn't even given Libby a chance to explain!

"And I thought my parents were strict," Libby mumbled to herself, brushing some of the dirt off her clothes. "Poor Julia." If Julia wasn't allowed to go outside, or talk to other kids after school, what kind of life did the poor girl have?

Libby quickly set the gloves and shovel on the Griffins' front steps, then headed for her house. Inviting yellow light shone from all the downstairs windows, a welcome sight against the darkening sky. When Libby stepped into her foyer, the warm, enticing smells of dinner and hot apple cider enveloped her. After dealing with Mrs. Griffin's arctic personality, it felt especially good to be home.

Once she'd finished dinner and gone upstairs, she made a concerted effort to put in a little study time. But even with Adam's earlier help, Libby still struggled with understanding some of her textbook. Long after her parents had stuck their head into her room to say good night, Libby finally gave up and let the textbook slip off her bed onto the floor. She flipped off her light and was about to close her eyes when the sudden sharp *ping* of something hitting her window jolted her upright. *Ping!* There it was again.

Libby jumped out of bed and peered out the window, trying to make sense of the shadows in the yard. Then one of the shadows moved, stepping into the moonlight and transforming into the very familiar outline of a certain someone with strawberry-blond hair.

Libby cranked open her window. "Nina!" she hissed into the darkness. "What are you doing out there?"

"Jailbreak." Nina giggled, opening a flap of her coat to reveal her pajamas and a large Ziploc bag. "I brought contraband. Are you going to let me in or what?"

Libby nodded and grinned, then tiptoed downstairs to open the door.

"Brownies," Nina whispered, holding up the bag under the porch light. "I made them this afternoon. With extra chocolate chips, just for you."

"Thanks," Libby said, thrilled that Nina was here with her, *and* that they were about to stuff themselves full of brownies. One of their favorite things to do together was make brownies (but they always ate at least half the brownie batter beforehand).

They hurried upstairs as quietly as they could, and once they were safe inside Libby's bedroom, they tucked themselves into Libby's window seat. Nina broke into the brownies, handing Libby an extra-large one.

"I decided two weeks was too long for you to go

without my brownies." Nina bit into hers and smiled. "And I know you're banned from hanging out after *school*. But technically, this is after *bedtime*, so I figured it doesn't apply."

"You're a lifesaver," Libby said through delicious mouthfuls. "I so needed chocolate today."

"I figured." Nina reached for another brownie. "How did it go with Adam, anyway?"

"Not too bad," Libby said. "He's actually pretty funny, in a goofy sort of way. And he did help me understand some stuff."

"That's good," Nina said. "Maybe the tutoring won't be as awful as you thought." She turned her brownie over in her hands, her face suddenly all seriousness. "You know, I was thinking about what you said earlier about Zack. And, well, maybe you're right. Maybe he's only being nice to me because I'm helping him with English." She tucked a strand of her hair behind her ear. "I guess I shouldn't read into it, right?"

The brownie Libby had just swallowed was sitting like cement in her stomach now. Nina was watching her face, waiting for a response, her eyes hopeful. "I think," Libby started, then faltered, searching for the right words. She didn't want to hurt

Nina's feelings again like she'd done before. That had been selfish of her, and she wanted to make up for it now. "I think I was wrong about what I said earlier. I mean, why shouldn't he want to talk to you?" She smiled and nudged Nina with her foot. "You're way more interesting than the Prim —" she caught herself "— most other girls. After all, now you're a global jet-setter *and* you're completely fabulous."

Nina beamed. "I don't know about fabulous, but I do make killer brownies."

"No doubt about that," Libby said. They grinned at each other, then hunkered down into the pillows with one more brownie each. They talked and laughed, and Libby felt waves of relief. There was no awkwardness here right now. Just two best friends having a good time, without Alia or Zack complicating things. It was perfect. Finally, when they were both stifling yawns, Nina stood up to go.

"Here," she said, tucking the bag of brownies into Libby's window seat. "You'll need these for sustenance while you finish doing your time in Mason Prison. When you get your freedom back, we'll make a double batch to celebrate."

"Thanks." Libby hugged her. "I'm so glad you came over. I really needed this."

"Me too," Nina said, then she tiptoed to the bedroom door. "I'll let myself out. I've got to get home before my parents figure out I'm gone, or I'll be grounded, too." She waved. "See you tomorrow."

Libby watched from the window as Nina sneaked back outside, climbed on her bike, and rode away. Leave it to Nina to end her dreary day on a fun note.

Libby glanced out the window again, this time studying the dark silhouette of the Griffins' house. It stood cold, gray, and silent among the trees, like a giant tomb. And Libby suddenly wondered if there was something she could do to cheer Julia up. After all, she was the new girl in town. She didn't know anyone here yet, and she had a strict, antisocial mother to boot. Maybe there wasn't anything wrong with her. Maybe she was just really lonely.

Well, if Julia didn't have a welcoming home, then Libby would see that Julia felt welcomed at school. She and Nina would make sure of it, starting first thing tomorrow.

CHAPTER FOUR

A sound, like an animal's claws ripping through wood, tore through her dreams. Libby's eyes flew open and she sat up, listening. There it was again. A faint but relentless scratching mixed with . . . crying? Libby's first thought was Nina. Had something happened on her way home? Had she come back? Libby opened her window, shook her drowsiness away, and peered out. Moonlight made a lacy patchwork of the dark, and there, kneeling in the grass of her front yard, was not Nina, but Julia. Her heavy hair hid her face, but her hands were working frantically, tearing into the dirt over and over again.

Libby checked the clock. It was one in the morning. What was Julia *doing* out there?

Libby tiptoed downstairs, grabbed her jacket and

Crocs, and slipped out the door. She gasped as the bitter air immediately turned her pajamas icy cold. Pulling her jacket tighter around her, she quick-stepped her way to the Griffins', her sockless feet already going numb. Julia was still on her knees, and her hair was dripping wet, just as it had been before. It clung to her face in ratty strands, mixing with the tears streaming down her sallow cheeks.

"Julia," Libby whispered, bending down over her, "what's wrong? What are you doing outside? It's *freezing*."

Julia didn't show any sign that she'd heard her at all. She kept on with her manic digging, and Libby could see her fingers were scratched raw and bleeding.

"Julia, please stop," Libby said. This was going from weird to scary in a hurry.

"I have to find it," Julia garbled through her sobs. She stared at the ground, but her eyes were vacant, unseeing. "I have to give it back to them."

"Give what back?" Libby peered at the ground, but all she could see was dirt and rocks. "To who?"

Julia's digging reached an almost hysterical pace. "It's still at the pond," she rambled. "I can't get it. They won't let me go." She moaned, covering her

face with her wrecked hands. "I'm trapped here . . .
forever."

Libby shook her head, trying desperately to
understand Julia's ravings. "What pond?" she asked.
"There's no pond around here. What are you trying
to find?"

No response.

"Can you even hear me?" Libby asked, but she
thought she knew the answer. Julia just kept staring
at the pathetic track marks in the dirt. It was like she
was sleepwalking, or in a trance. "Julia —"

A blinding light sliced through the darkness, and
Libby squinted at the Griffins' front windows, now
ablaze. Julia gasped and jumped to her feet. Without
another word, she scrambled around the side of the
house just as Mrs. Griffin threw open the front door.

"Olivia?" Mrs. Griffin marched down the walk-
way, waving a flashlight. "What on earth are you
doing?"

"I'm so sorry," Libby started, ready to explain
what she'd seen and Julia's insane behavior. It was
on the tip of her tongue. But the memory of Julia's
tortured, panicked face stopped her. Libby was suddenly sure that whatever Julia had been doing, it
needed to stay a secret. At least for now.

"Well? What happened?" Mrs. Griffin snapped, shaking her head in disgust as she examined the torn-up ground before her. "Look at this grass! It's ruined!"

"I . . . I lost my watch!" Libby stammered. "This afternoon when I was mulching, my watch must have fallen off. I came back to look for it. . . ."

"In the middle of the night?" Mrs. Griffin stared at her skeptically.

"I really am very sorry." Libby's face burned, and she hung her head. "It won't happen again." She knew how ridiculous the whole thing sounded. Her only hope was that Mrs. Griffin would let her go out of sheer exhaustion.

And sure enough, after an excruciating silence, Mrs. Griffin threw up her hands in disgust and defeat. "Well, you'll have to clean up this mess when you come back later."

"Of course," Libby muttered.

Mrs. Griffin sighed, then snapped off her flashlight. "Good night, Olivia."

"Good night," Libby gushed with relief, then hurried back to her house before Mrs. Griffin could do more scolding. It took a good fifteen minutes for her hands and feet to defrost under her comforter, and the whole time Libby replayed Julia's words again and again in her head. Was Julia really trapped? By what? Or whom?

She lay awake for hours, but no matter which way Libby spun it, none of it made any sense. When she finally drifted off it was into a disturbing semi-sleep. In her dreams, Julia was digging with jagged yellow claws, churning up a freshly dug grave.

Libby's eyelids drooped, and her head slumped slowly forward and would have hit her desk if a sharp elbow hadn't jabbed her in the ribs, jolting her awake.

"Snap out of it, Sleeping Beauty!" Nina hissed through her teeth. "Mr. Woodrow almost caught you that time."

"Thanks," Libby whispered. She shifted in her desk, forcing herself to sit up as straight as possible. But she could already feel the blanket of sleep smothering her again.

This time, it wasn't Nina, but the bell that shocked Libby into consciousness. She stifled a yawn and slid her math notebook into her bag, thankful she'd made it through first period. Now, if she could just stay awake through the other six . . .

"What is up with you today?" Nina asked as soon as they were out of Mr. Woodrow's earshot.

"I didn't get much sleep last night," Libby muttered. She scanned the faces in the hallways, just like she had this morning before classes started. But there was no sign of Julia anywhere. Waiting for the bus in her driveway that morning, she'd chanced a glance at the Griffins' house. The curtains fluttered for a brief second in that upstairs window, Libby saw a flash of raven hair, and then . . . nothing. And now Julia was MIA in school again, too. "After you left last night, I had this complete twilight-zone encounter with the girl from next door."

"Mmmm." Nina nodded. She whipped out her cell phone and began texting with lightning speed. "That sounds weird."

"Definitely," Libby said, and she quickly told Nina all about Julia's midnight escapade, and Mrs. Griffin's harsh treatment. "I know I shouldn't butt in, but I just feel like there's something strange going on. Julia's really scared. And she acts like she's not allowed to leave the house. Maybe something's really wrong."

"Huh," Nina said flatly while her thumbs flew over her keys. She glanced up for a millisecond before diving back into the texting. "It does sound like Mrs.

Griffin is a control freak for sure. Not unlike *your* mom." She shrugged. "You're flunking science and grounded for two weeks; maybe Julia's flunking something, too. I'm sure her mom has a reason for keeping her in the house."

"But last night, Julia said she was trapped. It's like — like she's a prisoner," Libby insisted. She wished Nina would put her cell away and focus, for just a second. Nina had been such a great listener last night, and they'd had so much fun talking. But now, Nina didn't seem even remotely interested in anything she was saying. "How can Julia be flunking school when she's not even *in* school?"

"Oh." Nina's thumbs froze while she gave that some thought. "Well, maybe she's homeschooled." Suddenly, Nina's phone vibrated. She glanced at the screen, then burst into bubbly laughter.

Libby sighed. It was no use talking to Nina when she was glued to her cell. She'd try to talk to her about Julia again at lunch maybe. "What's so funny?" she asked, at least hoping to get in on the joke.

"Oh, um, nothing," Nina said, but her cheeks darkened to cherry. "Zack just sent me a picture of his hamster dressed up like Shakespeare. You know, 'cause we're reading some of the sonnets right now in English." She looked absently at Libby, then waved her hand dismissively. "Never mind, you have to know the whole story. It's hysterical."

"Okay," Libby said, waiting for Nina to spill the rest of the story. But Nina didn't. She was already busy texting a response back to Zack with single-minded focus.

Libby rummaged through her locker, pretending to be very busy looking for something. It was easier to look distracted than to stand there feeling completely left out of Nina's little chat session with Zack. She quickly glanced in the mirror glued to the inside of her locker, taking in her honey-colored hair, the smattering of faint freckles across her nose, her hazel eyes. Her mom had once said that Libby had a sweet, fresh face, like she was a piece of fruit or something. But now, Libby studied Nina's delicate features in the mirror — the glossy hair, rosy skin, and striking eyes. It was no wonder Zack had noticed Nina and not her. Nina was noticeable. Libby was . . . nothing special.

Libby sighed, closed her locker, and turned to Nina. There was no point in putting off the inevitable. If Nina was crushing on Zack, Libby wanted to deal with it now and get it over with. She'd try to be happy for Nina. She'd *have* to be happy for her. She wouldn't be a very good friend otherwise. And besides, Libby couldn't and wouldn't do anything to keep Zack and Nina apart. Zack didn't even know who she was.

"So," Libby started, fumbling with the zipper on her bag, "about Zack. I want you to be totally honest with me." She swallowed. This was going to be tough to hear. "Do you like —"

"Nina!" a lilting voice rang through the hallway. "There you are!" A breathless Alia rushed over to Nina, followed closely by Selene and Vera, her girls-in-waiting. Alia flipped her blond locks over her shoulder and slipped a bangled arm possessively around Nina. "I *have* to tell you what I just heard!"

"It's about Zack," Selene squealed.

"Really?" Nina said. And then — yes — she actually squealed. Libby gawked at her friend. If there was one thing Nina was not, it was a squealer. Suddenly, her BFF was developing an alter ego right in front of her eyes.

"Shhh," Alia whispered. She leaned conspiratorially into Nina. "For your ears only."

Then Alia turned to Libby. "Sorry, but we need to borrow Nina for one sec. She'll be back soon. Promise."

Libby opened her mouth, but there wasn't time for anything to come out of it before Nina was whisked off to the bathroom in a tangle of giggling girls. Libby didn't know how long she stood there, staring at the bathroom door, before she realized Dee and Aubrey had come to stand beside her.

"Did I just see Nina get inducted into Alia's gossip group?" Dee asked.

"I think so," Libby said flatly.

"Our little Nina," Aubrey said, sniffling with exaggerated drama. "She's left the nest." Then she must have picked up on the annoyance on Libby's face, because she tucked her arm into Libby's. "Don't worry, she'll be at lunch, same as always."

"Maybe," Libby said quietly. Then the bell rang, and after some last-ditch efforts to cheer Libby up, Dee and Aubrey hurried off to class. Libby was left alone in the hallway, staring glumly at the pumpkin-hued posters of the Harvest Festival that had just been pinned on the hall bulletin board. And it suddenly dawned on her that, even if she pulled up her science grade and made it to the festival, she might not have a best friend to go with. And that thought set up camp and stayed, through an awkward, mostly silent lunch with Nina, through her tutoring session with Adam (despite the delish chocolate he brought), and far into another sleepless night.

By Thursday after school, Libby's mood mirrored the weather — gray and brooding. She gazed up at the thickening blanket of clouds and shivered. Then, she pulled more daffodil bulbs out of the bag and dropped them into the hole she'd dug. There was frost in the forecast tonight, and Mrs. Griffin had wanted her to plant the bulbs before the ground froze for good. Plus, Libby had promised to clean up the garden after Julia's delirious midnight dig. It felt good to do some physical work after maxing out her brain during Adam's tutoring sessions.

Today had been their third and last session for the week, and Adam had surprised her with a pop quiz on atoms, ions, and molecules. To her shock (and Adam's, too, she thought) she hadn't done too badly. Adam was actually turning out to be a pretty good tutor, and a fun one, too. He had ways of teaching her things that made them stick, like today's game of atomic bingo. There were worse ways to study science, Libby was sure.

Libby put the last of the bulbs in the ground, then rang the Griffins' doorbell, hoping that maybe Julia would be the one to answer it. But Mrs. Griffin answered the door, cool and frowning as usual.

"All finished," Libby said, trying to be nonchalant as she peered over Mrs. Griffin's shoulder into the stark white entryway. No sign of Julia anywhere, and the house was too still, too silent.

"Here you go, then." Mrs. Griffin handed Libby a ten-dollar bill. "Thank you."

She had already begun to shut the door, but Libby took a step toward her, and Mrs. Griffin froze, eyebrows arched in surprise.

"Mrs. Griffin," Libby persisted, knowing now was her chance to get to the bottom of things, once and for all. "I was just wondering if there was anything I can do for Julia. You know, if you want me to pick up some schoolwork for her to do, or anything. Until she starts school here . . ." Libby's voice died as she watched Mrs. Griffin's face go from pale to positively corpse-like.

"Mrs. Griffin, are you all right?" Libby asked, reaching out to steady her in case she was about to faint.

Mrs. Griffin seized the door like a lifeline. "What did you say?" she whispered. "How do you know my daughter's name?"

"Julia? She told me," Libby said. "I was talking to her the other day in the yard. When you thought I was on my cell —"

"How dare you mention her to me?" She clutched her throat like she was in physical pain. "What kind of cruel joke are you playing?"

"N-none," Libby stammered, heat flooding her face. This was going very, *very* badly. What was Mrs. Griffin talking about? "I'm not playing a joke, Mrs. Griffin. I wouldn't . . . I'm sorry I —"

"You should be," she snapped. "You have no right to talk about Julia. She's . . ." Her voice broke, and she covered her eyes. "My daughter is gone. She's been gone for a long time."

Libby stared. That wasn't possible. It couldn't be. "But, but I've seen her!" Libby shook her head, trying to clear the tornado of confusion from her mind. "I've —"

"Stop! Please stop now!" Mrs. Griffin held up her

hands, and Libby was mortified to see tears in her eyes. "I won't hear anymore." She swiped angrily at her eyes and straightened up, glaring at Libby. "I won't be needing your help with the yard anymore. Just . . . go home. And please don't come back."

The door snapped shut, and Libby stood frozen, dazed and trembling. How could Mrs. Griffin refuse to talk about her own daughter? And what did she mean, Julia was gone? When Libby was finally able to move, she walked slowly on shaky legs back to her house, then collapsed onto her bed. She had no idea what had just happened, but she was sure about one thing: Something was horribly wrong with the Griffins, and Libby was going to find out what.

CHAPTER FIVE

Libby reread the words in the textbook in front of her again, hoping this time they would actually sink in. But even though she tried to distract herself, the memory of her encounter with Mrs. Griffin had a vice grip on her brain. She'd wasted most of Saturday sitting at her bay window under the guise of studying, when really she'd just checked and rechecked the Griffins' house for any signs of life. But Julia had disappeared. The curtains at her window hung motionless, the room stayed dark. Mr. Griffin, who looked about as cheery as Mrs. Griffin, made a grocery run on Saturday afternoon, but that was the only movement at all at their house all day. Then this morning, a black car pulled into the Griffins' driveway, and a middle-aged woman with what looked like some sort of medical bag stepped out. Mrs. Griffin let her in quickly, and an hour later the woman left.

Since then, Libby had staked out her post at the window again and had been speculating on what the appearance of the doctor lady could mean. Was Mrs. Griffin physically sick? Or mentally ill? That could explain her odd behavior, and possibly Julia's. Maybe Julia stayed home to help take care of her mom, and had her own private tutor or something. But then, that didn't explain what Julia was looking for outside, or why she always seemed frightened and disappeared whenever Mrs. Griffin showed up. No, Libby's gut told her there was something more disturbing going on. What if Mrs. Griffin had done something to hurt Julia? What if . . . Julia was in some kind of real danger?

"Are they burying someone in their backyard over there or what?" a voice said behind her, and Libby nearly fell off the window seat.

"Mom!" she squeaked. "You scared me!"

Her mom gave her an apologetic smile. "I'm sorry. I thought you'd heard me come in. I promise to do better about knocking." She leaned into the window seat, peering out. "So, what exactly is so fascinating about the Griffins' house? You haven't left this seat since Friday night."

Libby shrugged. "Nothing. Just daydreaming. I'm fine, Mom. Really."

"Okay." Her mom straightened. "I just wanted to let you know that Adam called for you a bit ago on the house phone. You said you were studying, so I didn't want to bother you. But he asked you to call him back."

"Did he say why?" Libby asked. She couldn't think of any reason Adam would need to call her on a Sunday afternoon, unless it was to check up on her studying (*joy*).

"You'll see," her mom chimed. A sly grin streaked across her face as she left the room.

"Great," Libby muttered under her breath. If her mom was in on it, it could only mean one thing: more homework. Reluctantly, she picked up her cell phone and dialed the number her mom had written down for her.

Adam picked up halfway through the first ring. "Libby?" he said.

"Hey," she said. "My mom said you called?"

"Yup," he said. "Are you still under house arrest?"

"Pretty much. The only time I see the light of day is going to and from school," she joked. "And when they give me my bread and water, of course."

Adam laughed. "Well, you owe me big-time. I just got you out on bail. The mall. Monday. Four P.M. Be there."

"No way," Libby said. "My mom would never agree."

"Well, she did twenty minutes ago," Adam said proudly. "I told her I thought a change of scene would be good, and that the mall was a good place to study the properties of matter. It's tough to argue with a child prodigy."

Libby laughed, and her heart picked up the pace at the very idea of an afternoon of freedom. "Wow. This is great."

"Our meeting is strictly academic in nature, you understand," he said, deepening his voice. "Purely studying going on. We cannot, under any circumstances, have any fun."

"Yes, sir," Libby played along. "Thanks, Adam."

"Sure."

Libby hung up the phone, smiling. By this time tomorrow, she'd be at the mall, surrounded by stores, music, and other human beings. No more staring at the four corners of her bedroom walls. No more obsessing about Julia. Tomorrow, she was going to forget everything (well, *except* the periodic table). For the first time in her life, she was actually looking forward to more schoolwork.

Libby took a long, savory sip of her chocolate-chip cookie-dough milk shake, relishing the tiny bits of chocolate melting on her tongue.

"So how's your first taste of freedom?" Adam asked, looking up from his cherry-vanilla shake.

"Delish." Libby grinned. Today, even the campy elevator music drifting through the mall sounded amazingly good to her. "This is a vacation compared to the last week."

"Yeah, well, don't get too comfy in that mass-produced plastic chair of yours," Adam said, tapping his science textbook. "We still have to talk about matter. This milk shake, for instance. Solid or liquid?"

Libby examined the thick goop oozing its way down her straw. "Both," she decided.

"I'd say plasma," Adam said, examining his own shake. "Too bad we can't get the shake cold enough for some Bose-Einstein condensate. Then we'd really see something . . ." His eyes glazed a bit, and his face took on a look of fierce concentration.

"Earth to Adam," Libby said. "I know you're tapping into abnormally large amounts of brain matter right now, but remember you're dealing with the scientifically challenged over here."

Adam blinked and shook himself, then grinned. "Sorry." He took another sip of shake. "Sometimes the world inside my head is just more . . . interesting, you know?"

Libby nodded. "I feel that way sometimes, too. Like when I'm reading. The world in the book gets into my head, and I just want to stay there with it. Sometimes I feel like I was born into the wrong century. Maybe I was supposed to be born in Victorian England in a damp, dark castle."

"Without surfing, computers, and molecular biology?" Adam actually looked a bit horrified. "I wouldn't last a day."

"Web surfing?" Libby asked.

"Are you kidding?" Adam scoffed. "*Surfing*, as in ocean, waves, wet suits. There are some great places along the Jersey Shore. I try to go at least a few times each summer. My dad and I go camping down there, and I usually bring a few friends."

"Wow," Libby muttered. "That's cool. I just never imagined . . ." She let her voice die, embarrassed to say what was on the tip of her tongue.

"What? That I can actually do something besides quantum theory?" He raised his eyebrows, and Libby shrugged, blushing. "I *do* have a life outside the lab, you know."

They looked at each other for a few seconds, and then they laughed. But Libby's laughter stuck in her throat when she glanced up and saw Nina walking through the food court, chatting cheerfully away with Alia and Selene. And just at that moment, Nina glanced her way and their eyes met.

They both smiled, but then there was a split-second hesitation before Nina walked over. And, was Libby just imagining it, or did Nina look embarrassed?

"Hi," Nina said, giving a strained, high-pitched laugh. Alia and Selene smiled politely and gave half-hearted waves. "What are you doing here?"

"Studying," Libby said. Oh, this was *sooooo* awkward. "What are you guys doing?"

Nina blushed. "Um, we're going to see *Blood Moon*. It just came out today."

"Oh yeah," Libby said politely. "I heard that was supposed to be good."

"Yeah," Nina said. "Listen, I'm sorry I didn't invite you. I would've. But I just figured you wouldn't be allowed to come. Or that you'd be too busy with your tutoring and everything."

"You could've asked," Libby mumbled, staring at the ground, anger simmering under her skin.

"What?" Nina asked, but there was a tone of accusation in there that meant she'd heard Libby's comment perfectly fine.

"Nothing." Libby refocused on her milk shake. "You should probably get back to your friends."

"Right," Nina huffed, glancing toward Alia and Selene, who were off to the side, clearly waiting on her. "I'll see you at school tomorrow."

"Yup. Enjoy the movie." Libby kept her eyes on the table until they'd moved safely away. Then she blew out an exasperated breath.

"Wow," Adam said. "That was tense."

"Unbelievable," Libby said, staring after Nina as she drifted down the mall corridor arm in arm with Alia and Selene. "I just don't get what's happening with her lately. She's just . . . different. *We're* different. And I don't know how to fix it."

"Maybe you're not supposed to," Adam said. "Maybe you should just try not to expect things to stay the way they were before."

"But she's the one who wants to change," Libby said. "Not me."

"But you can't stop her from changing," Adam said matter-of-factly.

"Oh, *never mind*," Libby blurted, blowing her hair out of her face. What did he know about her friendship with Nina, anyway? Not a single thing. "Forget it. Let's not talk about it anymore."

"Okay." He shrugged, then looked seriously at Libby. "I am sorry about what's happening, though. Best-friend stuff is tough."

There was a real sincerity in his eyes that made Libby suddenly, inexplicably blush. For the first time, she saw what an unusual, overcast blue his eyes were — an indigo sky peppered with gray. How hadn't she noticed them before? They were actually — dare she even think it? — kind of cute. "Thanks," she said. Then she straightened her shoulders and stabbed her finger at her textbook. "Now, let's discuss what *matters*."

Adam blinked, then a slow grin eased onto his face. "Wait a minute. Was that a science joke?"

Libby smirked. "Maybe."

"It was a *really* bad one."

Libby laughed. "I knew you'd appreciate it. Now let's study before my mom picks me up. We don't want her to think we were sitting around drinking milk shakes the whole time."

"We would never do anything like that," Adam said. Then they grinned at each other and bent over the textbook.

By the time her mom picked her up an hour later, Libby had gotten a decent amount of studying done. And as she stared out the window of her mom's car, watching houses and streets fly by, she wondered if she'd misjudged Adam. Sure, he had his nerdy side, but there was so much more to him than that. Like the surfing thing . . . who knew? And he was funny, and pretty laid back for someone as smart as he was. And then another thought occurred to her. If she'd been misjudging Adam, maybe she was wrong about Nina, too. Maybe Nina was the one who was feeling left out. After all, it was Libby who'd been consumed with studying and the Julia mystery this past week. Wasn't it possible that Nina was missing their girl time just as much as Libby was? And maybe that was why she'd been hanging out with Alia so much?

Well, if that was the case, then Libby was going to fix it. She was going to forget about the Julia thing once and for all. And first thing tomorrow morning, she'd have a heart-to-heart with Nina and tell her how much she'd missed her and how sorry she was that they hadn't been able to hang out more. And as soon as she'd served her two-week sentence and passed her next science test, everything would be back to normal. It had to be.

CHAPTER SIX

The freezing, inky water was up to her ankles, and it was rising fast. Libby peered down the stark white hallway. Dark corridors split off the hallway in a mazelike puzzle, and there were so many doors. And she needed to find something . . . she just couldn't remember what. . . .

"Libby!" A frantic, hollow voice echoed off the walls. "Come find me, Libby!"

Julia. The voice was far away, hidden somewhere in the recesses of the flooding corridor, but it was Julia's.

Libby waded through the water, peering through an open doorway into an empty room. *Slam!* The door shut in her face.

"Hurry!" Julia cried feverishly. "Please! Before it's too late!"

Libby started running, kicking water up into her face as she did, lurching from room to room. By the time she reached the end of the hallway, she was dragging her feet like anvils, plunging her entire body forward with the effort to move.

The black water poured out of the last room, and it was inching its way up to Libby's waist now. From the hallway, Libby could see into the room. Julia was tied to a bed that was almost completely submerged, and she was craning her neck to keep her head above the rippling blackness.

Libby scrambled toward the room, crawling on her hands and knees through the water. She reached the doorway, then — *bang!* — the door slammed shut in her face. She threw herself at the door, pounding it with her fists, kicking it, anything to get it to open.

Then she heard it — the choking and coughing from the other side of the door. She could almost see Julia's face slipping under the surface, her eyes wide with terror, her mouth open in a gasp. Libby tore at the door, her hands burning with pain now. Finally exhausted, she collapsed against it. On the other side of the door, the coughing died, and an ominous silence remained. That's when Libby screamed.

She was still screaming when her eyes opened onto her sun-drenched room. Her sweat-soaked pajamas clung to her, her face was streaked with tears, and her heart was trampling her lungs with its manic hammering. It had all been a dream.

She brushed a hand across her clammy face. The water, the room, the horror splayed across Julia's face — none of it was real. Libby slammed her fists into her mattress. No! It was more than a dream. Julia was in trouble. And Libby was going to prove it.

She leaped out of bed, flew down the stairs and out the front door, not even giving herself time to think. The terror of the dream still gripped her, and even the shards of frostbitten grass jabbing her bare feet as she ran couldn't slow her down.

She reached the Griffins' and hurtled through the open front door into the foyer.

"Julia!" she screamed. "Julia, where are you?"

A spiral staircase was in front of her, and she took the stairs two at a time at a full-out run, only stopping when she collided with Mrs. Griffin at the top. Mrs. Griffin grabbed her firmly by the shoulders, and Libby vaguely registered the crumpled, untied bathrobe she must have thrown on hurriedly over her own pajamas.

"What on earth?" Mrs. Griffin asked breathlessly, her sleep-worn face riddled with fear and confusion. "What are you doing here?"

Libby threw off Mrs. Griffin's hands, jerking away from her. "I know she's here," she said, trying to step around Mrs. Griffin to move into the upstairs hallway.

"What's going on here?" Mr. Griffin said, rounding the corner of the upstairs hallway to come stand beside Mrs. Griffin. He was in his robe, too, and looked completely confused.

"You told me she's gone." Libby fired the words at Mrs. Griffin. "But she's not! I know I've seen her! You keep her locked up in this house all day long. She's never allowed to leave."

Mrs. Griffin's face crumpled into a mass of tired tears. "Locked up?" she repeated through sobs. Mr. Griffin wrapped his arm protectively around her.

"I think there's been a misunderstanding," he said quietly. "Olivia, why don't you have a seat." He motioned to a decorative bench along the upstairs hall wall. "I'd better call your parents, and then we'll all have a nice, calm chat."

Libby hesitated. She wanted to tear the entire house apart until she found where they were keeping Julia hidden. But Mrs. and Mr. Griffin stood together on the stairs like a fortress, and she saw there'd be no going anywhere anytime soon. She'd burst into their home and accused them of keeping their daughter a prisoner. There was no escaping this one. She grudgingly sank onto the bench, waiting for the other shoe to drop.

And five minutes later, it did, when her mom and dad tentatively walked in, looking embarrassed in their disheveled, early-morning hair and robes. But when they saw Mrs. Griffin's tear-streaked face, and Libby frowning on the bench, their embarrassment changed to concern.

"Libby?" her mom asked, rushing up the stairs to her. "Are you all right?"

"I'm sorry to disturb you both so early in the morning," Mr. Griffin started. "But there's been some confusion." He looked at Libby. "Maybe you'd like to try to explain?"

Libby stood up, her mind reeling with frustration.

"They have a daughter," Libby began haltingly. "Her name is Julia. I've met her. Talked to her. But Mrs. Griffin keeps saying that it's impossible. I know she's here in this house somewhere. I think she's hurt, and maybe even in danger. . . ."

"Libby, what are you talking about?" Her mom's face was white with worry.

"I know it sounds crazy," Libby gushed, her words picking up speed. She had to make them understand. "But I've seen her outside, in the garden. She's scared to leave the house. Maybe she's scared of what *they* might do to her." She tilted her head toward Mr. and Mrs. Griffin.

"Olivia!" her father said in a low, commanding voice. "What a horrible thing to say! Apologize right now!"

"No!" Libby said firmly. "I know something's wrong here. I don't care if you don't believe me."

Her mom and dad stared at her, completely mortified. And even she could scarcely believe that she was actually saying these things. It wasn't like her to disobey her parents, or to even argue with anyone. But she couldn't stop herself. She had to do this for Julia. "I know she's here. She *has* to be here."

After a moment of stilted silence, Mrs. Griffin cleared her throat and stepped forward. "You're right, Olivia. *Part* of her is here."

Libby's heart caught in her throat. "What do you mean . . . part of her?"

Mrs. Griffin let out a world-weary sigh, her face wilting with sadness. "Please, will you follow me? I'd like to introduce you to our daughter, Julia."

Mr. and Mrs. Griffin led them from the upstairs landing down a hallway to the right. When Libby stepped into it, she gasped. The mazelike corridors branching off the main hallway, the row of doors — all of it was exactly like her dream. And there was the last door at the very end of the hall, closed and waiting . . . for her. Before Mrs. Griffin even started toward it, Libby knew that was where they were going. She was sure now. There was no question. It had to be . . .

"Julia's room," Mrs. Griffin whispered, her hand on the doorknob.

Libby braced herself as Mrs. Griffin turned the knob, then stepped into the room. Suddenly, she didn't want to know the truth anymore. She wanted to get away, to run as fast as she could to anywhere but here. But her feet moved mechanically toward the open doorway, forcing her body forward.

And there, in her room, was Julia, with the same pallid, drawn face, black hair, and bottomless eyes. She was sitting propped up against pillows in bed, her legs tucked under a trendy lavender duvet that seemed out of place among all the strange medical equipment and medicines that surrounded the bed like a mini-ER. She lay there, unmoving, staring vacantly out the window.

"Julia?" Libby whispered, tentatively walking closer.

"She can't hear you," Mrs. Griffin said, her voice breaking. "She's not here . . . not really. Her mind is . . . somewhere else."

"I'm so sorry," Libby heard her mom say, and after that she vaguely registered her parents in quiet conversation with the Griffins, apologizing for all of the conclusions Libby had jumped to. Libby's mom mentioned something about Libby's obsession with gothic novels, and that all that reading must have let her imagination run a bit wild.

"But . . . what happened to her?" Libby finally managed to eke out.

"There was an accident," Mr. Griffin said. "About six months ago now."

"Julia and a friend were riding their bikes near a pond in our old town," Mrs. Griffin said. "We're not entirely sure what happened, but both girls ended up in the pond. The other girl must have gotten a cramp or something. We think she must have panicked, and Julia tried to help her." Mrs. Griffin shook her head, wringing her hands uselessly. "It was a horrible tragedy, but the other girl . . . well, she drowned. And Julia has been like this ever since."

Libby stared at Julia, trying to imagine the terror she must have felt that day, and the guilt. A thousand questions raced through her mind, but the words wouldn't come.

"Was she hurt in the accident?" Libby's mom finally asked.

"Not physically," Mrs. Griffin said. "She can eat and drink when we offer it. But she can't — or won't — speak or move. The doctors say she's in shock. They're calling it a catatonic state. She's disconnected from reality."

Mr. Griffin gently slipped his hand over Julia's, but Julia didn't blink or move a muscle. "We moved here because we thought a new town, a new house might snap her out of it," he said. "But so far . . . nothing."

"I'm sorry, Olivia," Mrs. Griffin said. "I may have been harsh with you a few times this week when I didn't intend to be. Sometimes it's hard for me to be around other kids Julia's age, because I want so much for her to be healthy, like you. And it was extremely upsetting when you told me you'd been talking to Julia outside the other day. I thought you were playing a cruel trick on me, because it's just . . . not possible." She glanced toward Julia, and tears welled in her eyes. "Julia hasn't left the bed since the accident."

"Is that true, Olivia?" her dad asked quietly. "Did you tell Mrs. Griffin that you'd been talking with Julia?"

Libby opened her mouth, then shut it again. What could she possibly say to them? That, yes, she'd had a chitchat with a girl who was clearly incapable of it? That she'd seen Julia walking — no, running! — more than once through her yard? Everything she'd seen and heard from Julia was impossible. Which meant she'd either imagined it, or . . . or what? Julia's ghost was haunting her?

Libby shook her head. No. This was all way too

crazy. Even if she tried to explain what had happened, no one would believe her. Why would they? Catatonic people did not run around outside and talk to their next-door neighbors. And neither did their ghosts. Did they?

"Well, Libby?" her mom asked. "Can you explain all of this?"

Libby pulled her eyes away from Julia's face. "Um, I can't," she mumbled. "I . . . must have been wrong about everything. I honestly didn't know anything about Julia's accident, and I never would've intentionally hurt your feelings, Mrs. Griffin. I'm so, so sorry for everything. I guess I was just . . . confused. I must have seen another girl in the neighborhood, or I thought I saw something and I really . . . didn't."

The eyes boring into her finally blinked, and the four adult faces collapsed into polite masks.

"Thank you for the apology," Mrs. Griffin said flatly. "And I'm sorry, too, if I seemed angry with you. I do know that imaginations can be powerful things." She smiled faintly. "Maybe not so many scary stories before bedtime anymore, right?" She exchanged a knowing-mother glance with Libby's mom, and her mom nodded.

Libby smiled, even though a bubble of anger was rising inside her. So now they were going to chalk everything up to too many ghost stories and talk about her like she was still in kindergarten?

"Well, it is Monday morning, and Libby's already going to be late for school," Libby's dad said, breaking the tension.

"Absolutely!" Mr. Griffin interjected. "You should be getting ready for your day." Both dads seemed relieved that the worst was over. "And no hard feelings, of course! Let's just start fresh and forget this whole unfortunate episode ever happened."

Libby allowed herself to be ushered toward the bedroom door between her parents, feeling like a prisoner being led to her cell. But while the adults continued their pointless small talk, Libby glanced back over her shoulder at Julia.

Julia's head had slipped on the pillow, so that now it was facing forward, away from the window. And Julia's eyes, intense and foreboding, were staring . . . right at her.

CHAPTER SEVEN

Libby's mom had to drive her to school since the bus had already come and gone. And, of course, as soon as they pulled out of the driveway, the interrogation began.

"Libby," her mom started, "this whole situation with the Griffins has your dad and me very worried. I know you love reading those dark mysteries, but I never imagined that you might mistake them for something that could happen in real life."

"Mom!" Libby glared at her. "This has *nothing* to do with what I read. This is different."

Her mom let a puff of air fill her cheeks before letting it out, exasperated. "Well, I'm just not sure what to make of all this."

"I'm sorry," Libby said quietly, turning toward the

window to escape her mom's worried gaze. "It was all a big mistake."

"It certainly was," her mom said. "Let me be absolutely clear with you. You are not to disturb the Griffins again. You need to be focusing on your studies and not on spinning wild tales about our neighbors."

"You're right," Libby said, knowing the best way to avoid more questions was to tell her mom what she wanted to hear. "I promise to leave them alone."

She could sense her mom was waiting for more, for a truth that maybe she hadn't been willing to admit in front of the Griffins. But Libby couldn't go down that road. It wouldn't help at all for her mom to think she'd gone off the deep end. She sighed heavily and began covering her tracks. "I guess . . ." Pause for dramatic effect. "I guess I've been kind of stressed-out lately. I've been studying so much, and I really don't want to disappoint you and Dad with another bad grade." She tried her best to look forlorn. "Maybe my mind just played a trick on me. I haven't been sleeping that well, you know."

Her mom looked relieved for a second, but then fresh concern erupted on her face. "Why didn't you say something, sweetie?" She gave Libby's hand a squeeze. "I have noticed how seriously you've been taking your studying." She patted Libby's knee with new resolve. "I don't think taking a little time off would hurt much."

"Really?" Libby said. Wow. She hadn't bargained for this nice perk.

Her mom slowed the car down to a stop in front of the school. "Why don't you see if Nina's around after school? The two of you can spend some time together just relaxing and having fun. I can take you somewhere, or you can hang out at home. And then you'll be all refreshed for your tutoring with Adam tomorrow."

Libby smiled. "That would be great. I'll talk to Nina about it later."

Her mom handed her a note to give to the office to explain her tardiness, and Libby gave her a quick peck on the cheek. "Thanks, Mom." Then, for good measure, she added, "Oh, and, please forget about the thing at the Griffins' this morning. It was stupid, and completely all my fault. But it's over with now. I promise."

"Good." Her mom's face lit up with a genuine smile. "I'll see you after school."

Libby kept her own smile pasted on as her mom pulled away, but it slid off her cheeks the second she walked into school. She let all of the confusion, humiliation, and fear of the morning's scene crash over her again as she remembered Julia's penetrating eyes burning into her. She could never admit this to her parents or the Griffins. But she knew beyond a doubt now, as she'd never known before, that her encounters with Julia were real, every one of them. She couldn't explain how they'd happened, but she knew there was a reason why. And she needed to find out what it was.

She picked up her tardy pass and sat through the remainder of her morning classes in a daze. When the bell rang for lunch, she went through the motions of collecting her things and walking to her locker. But Julia was all she could see, all she could think about.

"Libby!" a voice practically yelled into her ear, and she jolted back to reality as Nina poked her in the ribs.

"Didn't you hear me calling your name?" Nina narrowed her eyes, peering at Libby's face worriedly. "Hey, what's wrong? Where were you this morning, and why do you look like you just saw a ghost?"

Libby opened her mouth to say that maybe she actually *had* seen one, but Nina kept on going.

"Never mind. It doesn't matter where you were," Nina rambled, then grabbed Libby's hand, nearly causing her books to spill. "You can tell me later. Because right now, I have huge news! It's incredible!" She squealed, jumping up and down. "Guess who asked me to the Harvest Festival dance? You are not going to believe it!"

Libby clutched her locker door as her heart plummeted six feet under. Oh no. This could not be happening. Not right now.

"Zack Northam!" Nina shriek-whispered. "*I* am going to the dance with *Zack Northam*!"

Libby swallowed thickly, and winced as the name wrenched her heart. She somehow managed a lifeless, "Um, that's nice."

"Nice? That's it?" Nina gaped at her. "You said it like I have three weeks left to live or something. Snap out of it!" She giggled. "It's fantastic! And now I get to go shopping for a dress!"

Libby nodded, feeling tears threatening her eyes.

"So," Nina rushed on, not even glancing at Libby but instead, checking her phone's calendar. "I really want to try to go to the mall this afternoon, first thing after school. I know you're still housebound, but maybe your mom could make an exception just for today?"

And there it was. The very thing Libby had been looking forward to — the chance to spend some time with Nina just like they used to. But now the anger churning inside her was threatening to boil over. Zack — the boy Libby had liked for four whole years! Zack liked Nina. It was just too much.

"I-I can't go with you," Libby stammered, hoping the quiver in her voice wasn't too obvious. "Sorry."

"Aren't you going to even ask your mom?" Nina pressed on. "She might say yes. You never know. . . ."

"It's not that," Libby said. Her eyes were burning with the effort of holding back the tears. "I'm just not in the mood."

Nina threw up her hands, glaring. "I don't get you, Lib. I thought you'd be happy for me. You've been so wrapped up in drama over your science test, and I've tried to be understanding about it. But you've been a downer all week."

"It's more than the test," Libby started. "There's been other stuff going on. . . ."

"Like what?" Nina crossed her arms, waiting. "I really wish you would tell me, because I'm getting a little tired of the 'poor me' routine."

"You're tired of *me*?" Waves of rage burst out of Libby, and her voice rose to a yell. "I'm not the one who's decided I'm too good to hang around with my real friends anymore."

"What are you talking about?"

"You know exactly what I'm talking about," Libby seethed. "You've been so preoccupied with Zack and Alia and your new social status that you haven't even bothered to find out what's been happening in my life. You can't put your cell phone down for two seconds to listen to anything I say."

"Oh, and you've been such a good friend lately, too," Nina huffed. "Ever since you flunked that test, you've dropped off the face of the earth. What was I supposed to do, sit around bored while I waited for you to finish studying? I'm allowed to hang out with other people, Libby. And if you weren't so scared of anything new, maybe you'd have fun meeting new people, too."

Libby slammed her locker shut. "I'll tell you what. You should go dress shopping with Alia, not me. You love spending time with her so much. And she probably has much better taste than I do."

"You're right, she probably does," Nina snapped, spinning on her heel. "And she's way more fun to be around right now than you!" she called back over her shoulder as she marched away down the hallway.

Libby grabbed her bag and just barely made it to the girls' bathroom before the tears overflowed. This had officially become the worst day ever.

She dabbed at her eyes with wads of tissues. Luckily, the bathroom had emptied out for lunch, and she took a good five minutes to take some deep breaths before braving the cafeteria. Making her face a calm mask, she sat down at the table with Dee and Aubrey.

"Hey!" Dee said. She peered at Libby from over the top of her glasses. "So what's up with you and Nina?"

"What do you mean?" Libby asked, playing stupid. Had Nina told them already about their fight?

"She means," Aubrey said, nudging her, "why is Nina sitting over there instead of over here?"

Aubrey pointed, and Libby followed the arc of her finger to the other side of the cafeteria, where Nina was sliding onto a bench next to Alia, Selene, and Vera. Unbelievable. Well, maybe Nina was where she belonged now.

"I really don't want to talk about it," Libby muttered. "Okay?"

Dee and Aubrey exchanged a look of surprise, but then Dee shrugged. "Okay," she said. "I hate to leave you by yourself here, but we're going to have to abandon you in a few minutes. We're doing our decorating shift today for the Harvest Festival."

"It's going to be amazing," Aubrey said. "You should see the red chandeliers Principal Stelson found at the consignment shop in Gentry. Very Bram Stoker . . ."

"I can't wait to see them," Libby said, but her voice fell completely flat. She pretended interest as Dee and Aubrey gushed about the colors and props for the dance, but hearing about it just made her feel worse. The haunted-castle theme had been her idea, and now she couldn't even get excited about it. If she made it to the dance at all, there was no way she'd be there with Nina now. What a disaster.

"Hey, do you want to come with us to help out?"

Dee said as she and Aubrey stood up to throw away their trash. "There is plenty of room for more volunteers."

"My shift is tomorrow," Libby said, pained at the thought of having to work side by side with Nina after their fight earlier. And there was no doubt she would be there, overseeing all the work. "But you guys have fun. I'll see you later."

She waved at them as they left, and then stared down at her remaining lunch. For the first time ever, she was eating lunch in the cafeteria completely alone. Suddenly, she was sure she felt everyone staring at her, everyone noticing how ridiculous she looked by herself. She grabbed her bag in a panic, dumped the rest of her lunch, and headed for the hallway. She still had ten minutes before the bell rang, but she could not stay in the caf a single second longer.

She replayed Nina's words in her head, wincing at the memory. *If you weren't so scared,* Nina had said. And maybe she was right. Maybe if she wasn't so scared of taking chances all the time, things would be different for her. If she were braver, maybe she'd be the one who Alia wanted to be friends with. If she were braver, maybe she wouldn't be a middling anymore. And then the really big one — the one that stung her gut every time she thought it. If she were braver, maybe she'd be going to the dance with Zack Northam instead of Nina. Maybe she would have spoken to him long ago. Maybe she would have charmed him just like Nina had. So many maybes, and none of them would ever come true.

But there was one thing she was sure of: From this moment on, she was done being scared. And if Julia was somehow trying to reach her, if she needed Libby's help, then Libby was going to do everything she could to help her. Even if it meant breaking rules. But first, she needed to tell someone the truth about what had happened with Julia — someone who just might believe her. And she knew who that person might be. She buried her sadness over Nina deep inside, straightened her shoulders, and walked to the science lab. She knew Adam would be there, and she had a question for him.

Three hours later, Libby stepped through the doors of the Whitford Community Library. Luckily, the library was only a five-minute walk from school, so she hadn't needed her mom to drive her. Although her mom had actually offered, probably because she was so shocked.

"Let me get this straight," her mom had said when Libby had called her after school. "I told you that you could take a break from studying this afternoon, and you're asking me if it's okay for you to spend the afternoon studying?"

"Yup," Libby said. "I think Adam and I should go over a few things again."

There was a moment of stunned silence from the other end of the line. "Okay," her mom finally said. "I mean — great! As long as you're not wearing yourself out."

"Nope," Libby said. "I think this will actually make me feel much better."

So now Libby dumped her bag in a study cubicle in the back corner of the library and waited. Soon she saw Adam scanning the cubicles for her, and she waved him over.

"I have to admit," he said, pulling up a chair next to hers, "when you walked into the lab at lunch today, I actually thought you might be joining the ranks of science lovers everywhere."

Libby laughed. "Sorry to disappoint you, but I'm not a convert. Normally, if I'm in the lab, something's on fire or exploding. I just knew I could find you there." She smiled. "Thanks for agreeing to meet me."

"Sure," Adam said. He started to pull out his science book, but Libby stopped him.

"No science right now," she said. Then, to Adam's look of surprise, she added, "There's something else I have to talk to you about. And I need you to tell me if there's any logical explanation for what's been happening to me."

Adam raised his eyebrows. "*Okay*," he said, "sounds interesting." He leaned forward. "So . . . what's going on?"

She took a deep breath, knowing that it was probably just as likely that he'd laugh her out of the library as take her seriously. Finally, she blurted, "Adam, do you believe in ghosts?" She closed her eyes, bracing herself for his laughter. But it didn't come.

"Whoa," Adam said. "I didn't expect you to say *that*." He looked at her quizzically. "Seriously?"

"Seriously," Libby said, her heart pounding.

Adam rubbed a finger across his right eyebrow, something Libby had seen him do during their tutoring sessions when he was concentrating. "Well, the scientific part of my brain says no. Ghosts can't exist."

He paused. "But, then again, there are almost always exceptions to every rule. So, I guess a part of me is also open to the possibility."

"Good," Libby said, relieved that he wasn't ripping apart the whole idea, at least so far. "Because I think I'm being haunted."

"Oh." Adam nodded. "You mean you want to blame a ghost for making you fail science?" His eyes twinkled.

"Very funny," Libby said, elbowing him. "No, I mean I'm being haunted by a girl. A girl named Julia."

Adam's face sobered, and then he said quietly, "Tell me the whole story."

And she did. From the moment the Griffins moved in, to the fiasco at their house this morning, Libby told him every single detail. And when she was finished, she held her breath, waiting for him to say something . . . anything at all.

He was staring at the ground, rubbing his eyebrow furiously. "So," he finally said, "you think Julia's getting out of bed when her parents aren't looking and wandering around outside?"

"No," Libby said cautiously. "I think maybe Julia's body is staying in bed. But her soul, or spirit — call it whatever you want to — is leaving her body." She studied Adam's face for any sign of skepticism, but he seemed to be taking her theory into serious consideration. "Do you think it's possible that some part of Julia is trying to reach me? Some spirit part that can travel away from her body for a few minutes at a time?"

The finger rubbing the eyebrow froze. "Maybe." He slowly nodded. "There are some things that science can't explain yet. But that doesn't mean we won't have an explanation someday. The mind is incredibly powerful. Maybe it can send messages when the body can't."

"Do scientists study these types of . . . supernatural things?" she asked.

"Sure they do," he said. "I remember reading an article in *Scientific Monthly* not too long ago about out-of-body experiences. Doctors can actually give patients the sensation of out-of-body experiences by electronically stimulating a part of the brain called the temporoparietal junction." He stopped and looked sheepishly at Libby. "Sorry. Getting carried away with the vocab. But anyway, Julia's case is different because *you're* the one seeing her out of body."

Libby nodded. "Whenever I've seen Julia, she's

always said that she can't stay for long, or she's not allowed to leave. What if she means that she can't leave her body for too long? Maybe if she did, her body would die."

Adam looked at Libby appreciatively. "That's not a bad hypothesis." He grinned. "Maybe some of my brilliant science teachings have actually sunk in."

Libby snorted. "Don't get carried away."

"There is one thing that's really strange to me about this whole story," Adam said. "Why do you think Julia's coming to you?"

Libby shook her head. "I honestly don't know. I mean, why wouldn't she go to her parents, who love her so much?"

"Maybe her parents are too sad to hear her. She might have chosen the one person who would actually listen to her." Adam's eyes stayed on Libby's face until she blushed furiously. "Maybe she just needs a friend."

"Thanks," Libby said, "but so far I haven't been a very good friend to her. I haven't helped her at all." She sighed. "I need to find out more about her accident. I thought I could check the library's periodical database while I'm here. Maybe the accident made the local papers."

"I don't remember reading anything about a drowning in the *Whitford Press*," Adam said. "Do you know where she moved from?"

"No," Libby said, "but we can look up her name and see what pops up."

"Hmmm, it's like trying to find the coordinates to a wormhole."

She shook her head. "Um, I have no idea what that means. Please translate into Libby-speak."

"It means it's probably pretty impossible, but worth a try." Adam stood up and gathered his things, then looked back at Libby. "Well, are you coming or not?"

Her hopes lifted. "You're going to help me?"

"Of course," Adam said matter-of-factly, as if the alternative wasn't even an option. "You've just presented me with a phenomenon that defies rational explanation. Maybe finding out what's happening to Julia could be my next science project." Then he smiled. "And . . . maybe I just want to help you, even if you do have a bad case of the crazies."

"Watch out," Libby teased. "It might be catching." They laughed, and relief swept over Libby. After all that had happened today, it actually felt great to lighten things up a bit, even if it was just for a few minutes. "Okay," she said, "let's see what we can find out."

Searching through the periodicals database didn't take as long as Libby had feared. Within ten minutes, she'd found two articles referencing a Julia Griffin. They were both from the *Brookdale Daily*.

"Brookdale," Adam said, reading the screen from over Libby's shoulder. "Is that the Brookdale that borders Whitford?"

"Yes," Libby said, adrenaline speeding through her veins. "I can't believe she lived in the town right next to ours." She clicked on the link to the article, and held her breath as she read the headline: TRAGIC DROWNING TAKES THE LIFE OF LOCAL GIRL.

This was the story she was looking for. It had to be. Her eyes raced over the first paragraph of the article:

Today the citizens of Brookdale mourn the loss of one of our own. Yesterday afternoon, eleven-year-old Kara Johansen drowned in a tragic accident at Raven Pond. She and her best friend, Julia Griffin, had biked to the pond for the afternoon. It is uncertain how both girls ended up in the frigid water, as there were no witnesses at the scene (Julia Griffin has been unable to comment on the events that took place). But it seems that Kara may have suffered a cramp while swimming and drowned. Julia was found a short time later by a jogger, sitting on the pond bank, nearly hypothermic and in shock. Autopsy results on Kara are pending, but police have no reason to suspect foul play of any kind.

"This was just a heartbreaking accident," Sheriff Townsend said. "Kara was a bright, wonderful girl who will be sorely missed."

The article went on to give the details of the memorial service that would be held for Kara, and where flowers and condolences could be sent.

"So it happened at Raven Pond," Adam said. "I know where that is. My dad and I went fishing there once."

"How awful," Libby said, rereading the story over again, searching for any more information she might have missed the first time. "Poor Kara and Julia."

"What does the second article say?" Adam asked.

Libby clicked on the second link, then caught her breath. "It's Kara's obituary," she said quietly. She printed both articles and slid them into her bag, then sat back in the chair, defeated. "That's it. We barely know any more than when we started."

"We know where it happened," Adam said. "That's a start."

Libby shook her head, disappointment biting into her. "There's more to the story than this," she said. "I can feel it." A vision of Julia digging through the dirt filled her mind. "There's something Julia's trying to find. Maybe it has something to do with the accident."

"Maybe," Adam said. "But I don't think we're going to find much else out here. You might see Julia again. . . ."

"I don't know about that," Libby said. "Her parents are probably getting a restraining order against me as we speak."

"Well, if Julia wants to reach out to you, she'll find a way," Adam said. "I don't think ghosts give up that easily." He looked at his watch. "It's almost six. Our parents are probably outside waiting."

"Oh my gosh, you're right. Let's go." Libby leaped to her feet and threw her things together. Then they made their way to the exit. Rain was pummeling the parking lot outside, and Libby could barely make out the blurred outline of her mom's car through the sheets of water. Adam grabbed an umbrella out of his backpack, and the two of them hurried into the downpour.

A few feet from her mom's car, Libby's feet hit a slick spot in the pavement. She lost her balance and started down, heading straight for a monstrous puddle.

"Hang on," Adam said, grabbing her quickly around the waist and setting her upright again. Then, just as quickly, he let go and shoved his hand in his pocket.

"Thanks," Libby said, grateful that the threatening sky could hide her crimson cheeks in darkness. "And thanks for tonight. For believing me."

"You're welcome," Adam said, smiling. "And listen, Libby. Don't give up on Julia yet."

"I won't," Libby said. She waved good-bye to Adam and climbed into the car.

"So, how did the studying go?" her mom asked. "Are you feeling better about things now?"

"Yes," Libby said, and she realized it was true. Even if she still didn't know what Julia wanted from her, at least she had someone that she could talk to about it. She shivered as the rain hammered the car roof, and wrapped her damp coat more tightly around herself. And then warmth flickered through her as she remembered Adam's arm holding her in the parking lot. She realized that she sort of liked the way his arm felt around her. Which was strange. After all, this was brainiac Adam she was talking about. But then again, there were a lot of strange things happening in her life these days. And she had a feeling that they weren't over yet.

CHAPTER EIGHT

The pond stretched before her like the wide, black mouth of a freshly dug grave. Icy thorns of water stabbed her feet and unseen grasses, like tiny fingers, slithered around her ankles. Libby wanted to run, but she couldn't. Extraordinary heaviness pulled at her limbs, paralyzing her. She was waiting, watching the bottomless water. Or . . . was something in the water watching her?

A stark white branch floated up from the depths. She reached out involuntarily, the same force that was holding her there now making her move against her will. Her hand closed around the strangely smooth limb. But it wasn't a branch. It was a human bone. And now the water was full of bones and other dead things drifting past her. A small, ragged bird with lifeless eyes. A bloated mouse.

Then, something bigger, rising up from the murky shadows, something taking the shape of a . . . of a . . .

Libby clamped her eyes shut. She didn't want to know what else was buried in the blackness. She fought to pull her legs out of the water, but a hand clamped down on her shoulder, and Julia was suddenly beside her. Her face was inches from Libby's, her eyes wide and intense. Her skin shone with a ghoulish pastiness; her hair dripped and tangled with water reeds.

"Come see," Julia whispered, and then she pulled Libby under.

Libby opened her mouth to scream, and the foul water rushed in, choking her. She twisted violently, but Julia's grip was fierce as chains.

Libby clawed hopelessly at the water, and then she froze. Because there it was — so close she could touch it. A young girl's body, gray and listless in the dark, entwined with serpentine grasses. Pale blond hair rippled around her head, hiding her face. Libby spotted a sudden shimmer of movement. No, a glint of light from just below the girl's bare foot. Libby craned her neck to see the silvery outline of a bracelet covered in algae and bottom sludge. She could just make out the tiny, delicate roses dangling from it.

But then the girl's face turned toward Libby, the chalky blue eyes staring in horror, the mouth split open in a silent scream.

Libby gasped, and the freezing water filled her lungs. Panic seized her and she thrashed wildly, but Julia's grip tightened, shaking her, drowning her . . .

"Libby!" A voice cut through the water from far away, and firm hands were on her shoulders, shaking her.

"No!" Libby screamed, fighting with all her strength.

"Libby, wake up!" The voice was louder, more insistent this time.

Libby sucked air into her burning lungs, and her eyes opened to stabbing brightness. She clenched them shut again, reeling through her heaving breaths.

"Are you all right, honey?" Her mom's hazy face slowly solidified. "That must have been quite a nightmare."

"Yeah." Libby slowly sat up, still feeling the wintriness of the pond even in the warmth of her bedroom.

Her mom smoothed the hair from her face, then kissed her forehead. "Well, you're safe now. None of it was real. But you know that." She smiled, then stepped to the door. "I made pancakes, when you're ready."

Once the door was safely shut, Libby collapsed against her pillow. *None of it was real.* Somehow, her body was having a tough time buying into that. The same horrific images shattered the calmness of her room and bombarded her mind — the cold, deadened eyes of the girl in the pond; the bracelet; Julia's looming, haunted face. Tremors of panic still shook her hands and her heart every few seconds. And . . . why was she so cold? It was then she realized it, and she slowly lifted the blankets that covered her.

Her pajamas, her sheets, her whole body was soaking wet. Her hair was waterlogged too. This wasn't possible. It couldn't be. It was almost like . . . almost as if . . . she'd gone for a swim.

*   *   *

Even into the middle of the day, Libby felt the dampness clinging to her. Spending her lunchtime painting bloody mummies and skeletons didn't help much to snap her out of her morbid mind-set either. Today was her shift working on the Harvest Festival decorations, and she was up to her elbows in glow-in-the-dark spiderwebs, black lights, and plywood coffins. And to make matters worse, Nina was on the other side of the gym with Alia and her girls, spray-painting Styrofoam tombstones and pretending like Libby didn't exist. They'd had an awkward eye-contact moment when Libby had first walked in, but after that Nina kept her eyes singly focused on the graveyard she was building.

Libby sighed and repositioned the ragged mummy she was painting in her lap. Then she cast another side glance at Nina. She was laughing and whispering something in Alia's ear. They looked inseparable, and Libby cringed.

"Don't worry about her," Aubrey said in a hushed voice, following Libby's gaze. She stapled some more red satin into the coffin she was working on. "She's going through a phase."

"Probably a permanent phase," Libby said, but she still smiled gratefully at Aubrey and Dee, knowing that they were only trying to help. They didn't even have to be here right now. Even though they'd already done their shifts yesterday, after she'd told them about her blowup with Nina, they'd offered to tag along with Libby for moral support.

"Don't assume anything, Libby," Dee chimed in now. "There's no rule that says she can't be friends with Alia *and* with us."

"You mean, there's no *spoken* rule," Libby said, but she had a feeling that the rule was there, just the same. Nina couldn't stay a middling and mix with the royalty — that just wasn't reality.

Libby dabbed a bit more red paint onto the side of the mummy's head, trying to make it look like oozing blood. Normally, painting gothic props would've been right up her alley. But with her own head filled up with bones and death, she couldn't take pleasure in any of these morbid decorations. They were just reminders of her horrible nightmare.

"You could go over and talk to Nina," Aubrey said to her. "Break the ice."

Libby shook her head. "I don't have anything to say to her," she said firmly, the lie gritty in her mouth as she said it. There was plenty she wanted to tell Nina — everything about Julia, and the dreams. But those were things Libby would tell her best friend, and she wasn't sure Nina fit that description anymore. Besides, right now Nina was way too wrapped up in her new social life to listen. She'd proved that yesterday.

Dee squeezed her arm. "She'll come around. You'll see." Then Dee suddenly looked right past Libby and sucked in her breath. "OMG, *he's* coming over here," she hissed.

"Who?" Libby whispered, but then she found herself face-to-face with the answer: Zack. He was standing right next to her. If she'd moved just an inch, their shoulders would have brushed. She held her breath. He was looking right at her.

"Hi." He smiled, and nodded politely to Dee and Aubrey. "Um, Lilly, right?"

"Libby," she managed to stammer, wondering if everyone in the entire gym could hear the obnoxious clattering of her heart. "I'm Libby."

"Okay." Zack's eyes skimmed around the rest of the gym, and Libby couldn't decide if he was checking to make sure no one was watching him chat with a middling, or if he was keeping his eyes moving constantly so that he wouldn't actually look like he *was* chatting with one.

"So, Libby, I know you're friends with Nina and all. I figured you could tell me what her favorite flowers are? I wanted to get her some for the dance."

Libby's hopes deflated. The only reason he was even over here was Nina. "Um, sure," she forced herself to answer. "Daisies. She really loves daisies."

"Thanks," he said. He started to turn away, then stopped, and wrinkled his forehead in distaste. "Man, these have to be some of the lamest props I've ever seen. What are they trying to make it look like in here, an episode of *Scooby-Doo*? Geez."

"It's supposed to look like the inside of an ancient castle," Libby said, a slight defensiveness creeping into her voice. "Something like Northanger Abbey, a castle from a Jane Austen novel."

"Forget Nottingham whatever," he said. "They should've gone with *Texas Chainsaw Massacre* instead. Now that would've been cool." He shrugged, already moving away.

Libby watched him walk through the gym doors, disappointment crushing her insides. "He doesn't like the theme," she whispered hoarsely.

"Who cares?" Aubrey said. "Not everyone's an Austen buff like you, Lib. He's way too pretty to be bothered reading classics."

Libby nodded, knowing it was probably true. But, still, her first real chat with Zack and she found out he thought her idea for the festival was lame? And he didn't even know *Northanger Abbey*? After all the times she'd pictured talking to him, her conversation with him hadn't been anything like she'd expected. Suddenly, the perfect Zack Northam of her daydreams developed the tiniest fissure cracks.

"I can't believe he asked you about flowers for Nina," Dee said. Her face took on a dreamy haze. "That is so sweet."

"Yeah," Libby said woodenly. This whole thing had given her an empty, deflated feeling, like no one really understood her at all. Not Nina, and definitely not Zack.

"*I* can't believe he talked to any of us," Aubrey said. "I thought we were just a bunch of nameless faces to him."

"Nameless faces," Libby repeated, and suddenly, lightning crackled in her head. Every face — even a waxy, lifeless one — had a name, an identity. It was just a matter of figuring out what it was.

Libby stuck her paintbrush back into the can of paint, and pulled off her smock. "Listen, would you guys mind finishing up for me?" she pleaded. "I know it's horrible that I'm bailing, but there's something I have to do before the bell rings."

Both her friends looked confused, but Dee nodded. "Of course we'll finish. No worries."

"Thanks," Libby called over her shoulder, already rushing for the door.

She half-ran through the hallways to the school library, checking her watch as she did. Just over five minutes before the bell. Hopefully that would give her enough time. She plunged through the library doors and made for the closest Internet kiosk she could find.

"Come on, come on," she urged as she waited for the Internet search engine to flicker onto the screen. There it was.

She quickly typed in: *Kara Johansen, Brookdale, NY.* Then she hit ENTER and waited. More than a dozen links popped up, blogs from Kara's friends about her accident, an e-article about it. But Libby was only interested in one thing. She clicked on *Images* in the search-engine task bar.

And there was the face she'd seen in her dream. The same wispy blond hair, the same heart-shaped face, the same blue eyes. Only the girl in these photos had shimmering, windblown, sun-kissed hair and lively, sparkling eyes. The girl in these photos was laughing, playing basketball, horseback riding. And — in one photo that stopped Libby cold — the girl beamed at the camera, arm in arm with Julia Griffin. An icy fist gripped Libby's heart as she stared at the online photos. The dead girl in Libby's dream was Kara Johansen.

Libby wasn't sure what happened when the bell rang — how she robotically made her way to her classes, pretended to listen and do her work, and got on the bus. She wondered how no one stopped her, how no one noticed what was happening to her. How no one could see that Julia was inside her, planting images in her mind of a dead girl she'd never met, let alone seen.

But when Libby stepped off the bus into her driveway, Russ, the driver, nodded and waved, just like he always did. And she waved back, her hand mechanically performing the routine. And even when she saw Mrs. Griffin pulling her car out of the driveway next door, she waved in her direction, too. Mrs. Griffin's eye flickered with surprise for a brief millisecond, and then she lifted her fingers off the steering wheel in a tentative greeting. Libby felt the corners of her mouth pull into an obligatory smile, as if everything was right with the world.

But it wasn't. Because when Libby glanced up at Julia's window, her smile turned frigid. Scrawled across the glass in bloody lettering were the words COME SEE.

Libby knew the message was meant for her. Julia was giving her clues, pieces of the story, one bit at a time. First the dream, and now this. Libby could barely steady her shaking hands long enough to read her watch: three thirty. Today was one of her mom's days in her real-estate office, so Libby had an hour before her mom would be home. And she'd just seen Mrs. Griffin drive away. Her chance was now or never.

She quickly crossed the Griffins' yard to their front door, casting glances down the street to make sure no neighbors were out who could catch her. Her fingers gripped the doorknob and turned, and just as she knew it would, the door opened. She listened for sounds of life, but the house was still and quiet.

She hurried up the stairs and down the hall to Julia's room. And there was Julia, a pale statue in her bed, vacant eyes turned unblinking toward the window. The sheets were folded neatly back over her legs — no wrinkled, chaotic tangles, no sign that Julia had moved at all.

But then she saw it. A thin tube of crimson lip gloss on Julia's nightstand. Libby carefully picked it up, turning it over in her hands. The color of the lip gloss matched the color of the words on the window. Libby searched Julia's face, looking for any sign of life in her eyes. But they stayed hazy and fixed. Was it possible that Julia had gotten up and written those words, even in this zombie-like state?

Libby cautiously sat down on the bed beside Julia.

"Come see what, Julia?" she asked. "Show me. Please. Help me understand."

Then she waited. Minutes passed. Two, four, eight, ten. And Libby sat, watching Julia's unchanging face, until she couldn't take it anymore.

"Ridiculous," she muttered finally, standing up to leave. "This is ridiculous. She can't do anything." Libby shook her head, silently scolding herself. She turned to the door, but a sudden, loud thud from behind her made her jump. She looked back, heart racing. But Julia hadn't moved. She peered around the bed, and spotted a book lying facedown on the carpet by the nightstand.

Libby picked it up, careful not to let it close, and turned it over. Swirling, girlish cursive filled the pages. It was a diary — Julia's diary.

Libby's heart was revving up now, and she peered more closely at the entry on the pages. It was dated April twentieth of this year. April twentieth — the day that Kara drowned.

Libby caught her breath, and began to read:

Every time I think about that awful bracelet, I'm tempted to call Kara and cancel our whole picnic. I know I probably shouldn't be so angry about it. But Kara loves it so much. I can see it on her face every time she looks at it shining on her wrist. Why did Heather have to give it to her? Heather, who's only been friends with Kara for a few weeks. Not friends since birth, the way Kara and I have.

That bracelet must have cost at least fifty dollars... maybe even more. Heather's dad must have forked over the cash without thinking twice (no measly five-dollar allowance for the girl who lives in a mini-mansion). She would never have thought of making Kara something homemade. Nothing as tacky as a seashell picture frame. What was I thinking? That picture frame was the stupidest gift ever . . . something a five-year-old would give to her mom. But even if it was stupid, why did she have to hide it like she was ashamed of it?

Yesterday when I was over at her house, I saw it shoved into her desk drawer. I pretended I hadn't seen it. I pretended that everything was okay, even though the jangling of that bracelet on her wrist was driving me up the wall. She told me she's been sleeping with it on, like she can't be without it.

I hate that bracelet. And I hate Heather for giving it to her. But . . . never mind. Today, I'm not even going to bring up Heather. It'll just be the two of us at the pond. And we can talk about everything, just like we used to. We're going to have so much fun. I can't wait.

Libby turned the page, but the rest of the diary was empty. April twentieth was the last entry in it. She stared at the words on the page, and an image of the rose bracelet lying at the bottom of the pond jolted her out of her trance. The bracelet that she had seen in her dream, coated in mud. It was real.

All of the missing pieces suddenly fell into place.

I have to find it, Julia had said that night she was digging in her front yard. *I have to give it back to them.*

Libby knew beyond any doubt now. The bracelet was what Julia was looking for, and it was still lost somewhere in Raven Pond.

She stood up and carefully set the diary on Julia's nightstand. Then, she leaned over Julia, putting a hand gently on her stiff shoulder.

"I'll help you," Libby whispered. "I promise."

She grabbed her bag and carefully made her way outside, making sure she'd left no sign that she'd been in the house at all. The brisk wind blew away the stale scent of Julia's sickroom, but Libby knew there was no escaping Julia. If Libby broke her promise, if she couldn't help Julia, would Julia torment her with nightmares about Kara forever? Would Julia waste away in that bed for the rest of her life, trapped inside a rigid prison of a body? Or, worse, what if Julia's spirit left her body again and never returned at all? No, Libby wasn't about to let that happen. She needed to make things right, for both their sakes. And she knew just how to do it.

She wasn't sure if it was the best idea she'd ever had, or the craziest. But either way, she knew she couldn't go through with it alone.

CHAPTER NINE

"That is definitely the craziest idea I've ever heard," Adam said. They were supposed to be sitting at the kitchen table studying, but once Libby had confessed her entire plan to Adam, the Wednesday tutoring session had gone out the window.

"Don't look at me like that," Libby said, dunking her head into her forearm. "You know it's logical."

Adam snorted. "Logical? Okay, let's break it down. First, we lie to your parents. Then, we leave town on bikes. Then, you go for an Icelandic swim, probably drown, and the police arrest me for murder. Does that just about sum it up?"

Libby grinned. "And they say left-brained people have no imaginations," she teased.

"This is not logic, this is delusion," Adam said.

"Of course when you say it like that it sounds insane. But in actuality, it all makes perfect sense."

And it did. She'd mapped out the plan at school that day, barely hearing a word that was said by any of her teachers. Under the guise of a study session, she and Adam were going to bike to Raven Pond on Sunday morning, and she was going to find Kara's missing bracelet. It was as simple as that.

"I've already talked to my parents, and they're okay with us meeting to study at the library on Sunday," she said. "They're worried about the test on Monday, anyway, so it's the perfect excuse."

"You mean the perfect *lie*," he said. "And they *should* be worried. Their daughter somehow thinks she can go diving in water that would make polar bears shiver."

"It's not going to be that bad." Libby shrugged. "I'm a good swimmer."

He leaned forward, all humor suddenly erased from his face. "Seriously, you're going to freeze out there. It's the end of October already. They're forecasting snow for next week."

"I'm not going to be in the water that long."

Adam was doing that rubbing thing with his eyebrow again. "But you don't even know where the accident happened in the pond, or how deep it is. You'll never find a tiny bracelet."

"I'm going to try," Libby said firmly. "And I have this weird feeling that Julia will help me. I don't know how, but she will if she can."

"Look, I believe in Julia. You know I do. But even if part of her is leaving her body for short spurts, Raven Pond is at least ten miles from here. It would be way too far for that kind of thing."

"You don't know that," Libby said, getting more and more insistent. "You said yourself that science can't explain everything." She looked down at her hands. "I trust her," she added quietly. "She won't let me get hurt."

"I don't like this. It's too risky." Adam frowned, shaking his head. "And what about your test on Monday morning? I haven't been tutoring you for the past two weeks straight just to have my efforts go wasted. If you get hypothermia, how are you going to chart the periodic table?"

"I'll be ready," Libby said with as much conviction as she could muster. But she could tell by the doubt in his eyes that he wasn't buying it. She blew out a breath and leaned forward, locking eyes with him. "Look, I'm going to Raven Pond on Sunday afternoon, with or without you. I need to do this, but I was hoping you'd come along. You're the only person I've told about all of this. *And*, I trust you more than I trust Julia." She offered him a little smile.

"Of course you trust the first available living guy over zombie girl. That's not even much of a compliment." Adam made a big show of grimacing, then rolled his eyes. "I guess I could look at it as a chance to study out-of-body experiences. If anything weird actually happens, that is. Maybe there's a future science experiment here somewhere."

Libby's smile widened. "So you're in?"

Adam nodded. "But you're wearing a wet suit. I have one you can borrow."

"Done." Relief swept through Libby, and she nearly jumped out of her seat to hug him. But she stopped herself, the thought of being that close to him making her blush. Then, the fact that she'd actually *wanted* to hug him made her blush even more. "Thanks, Adam," she finally managed to stammer.

"Don't thank me yet." He jabbed a finger at the science textbook. "We are doing some big-time prep work for the test. Starting right now. You're acing this test. You owe me that much."

Libby nodded. "Give me my orders, sergeant. I'm at your mercy."

Then she gladly opened her textbook. It was the least she could do for Adam. Because even though she'd told him that she would go to Raven Pond without him, she didn't want to. And now that Adam had agreed to go, there was no turning back.

The rest of the week was a blur. At least Thursday and Friday Libby had school as a distraction, even if she could barely manage to focus. She spent half her time in class thinking about the pond — what it would look like, how cold the water would be, and (the question that pulsed pricks of panic through her veins) what she would find in its depths. The other half of her time she spent trying her best to avoid Nina. And as far as she could tell from the rare glimpses she caught of the back of Nina's head, Nina was doing the same.

They hadn't spoken to each other since their fight on Monday, and as far as Libby could remember, it was the longest stretch they'd ever gone without talking. Even when Nina had been in Italy for those three months, they'd texted and emailed and talked, and even Skyped a few times. Not to have Nina to turn to right now, to share what was happening with Julia, was the worst part of it all.

As Friday turned into a painstaking Saturday, Libby kept wondering what Nina would think about her plan. What would she say about Julia now? Would she have agreed to come to the pond if Libby had asked her instead of Adam, and cheered Libby on in traditional, peppy Nina fashion? Or would she have laughed at Libby and told Alia how relieved she was to be rid of her crazy former BFF? Libby used to be able to predict what Nina would say or do with amazing accuracy, because she knew her so well. But now it seemed like that was over.

Still, when she didn't have anything to distract her from the fear hacking away at her insides, she missed Nina even more. Twice she even absentmind-edly picked up the phone and started to dial her number. It was out of sheer habit, but she caught herself in time and hung up, reminding herself that Nina didn't have any real opinion about Julia at all because she'd never bothered to listen. Nina, she decided, didn't care. And that was that.

Sleep wouldn't even come to give her a break on Saturday night, and when the first rays of sunlight sluggishly peeked between the trees in her backyard Sunday morning, Libby was showered, dressed, and ready. Breakfast with her parents was torture, as she guiltily crafted one lie after another about her study session with Adam. If they ever found out the truth about where she was actually going today, she would never see the light of day again. But somehow, she survived the meal, and by nine she was standing outside the library doors, waiting.

Five minutes passed, and doubt itched at her mind. What if Adam didn't show? What if he had decided this was all completely insane? But then . . . there he was, zipping his bike up next to hers, smiling that quirky sideways smile she'd gotten used to.

"You're late," she said.

"I was building up suspense," he said, eyes sparkling. "It makes my entrance more dramatic."

"I don't need any more suspense today, thanks."

"Okay, okay, sorry. The truth is, I forgot the wet suit and had to go back for it." He patted the backpack slung over his shoulders. "I packed some food, too. I figured we might not be back until after lunch at the earliest."

"Good idea," Libby said. Leave it to Adam to think of everything. He was such a good friend. Her mind froze, hitting pause on that thought. A friend? The realization suddenly dawned on her that — yes — he had definitely become a good friend. She wondered what would happen after her test tomorrow. Would Adam still be her tutor? She hoped so, because if he wasn't, she was actually going to miss him.

She took a deep breath, burying that depressing thought. "I guess we're ready, then."

The ride was pretty, especially once they left Whitford — a quiet, winding road that passed horse pastures and lovely stone colonials and then rambled through light-streaked pine and birch trees. The air was brisk on her cheeks, though the sun added a hint of welcome warmth. But when they rode past a signpost that said, RAVEN POND, 1 MILE, everything changed.

The pillowy white clouds that had been scattered across the blue sky slowly fused into a thick, steely blanket. A bitter wind picked up, whipping strands of hair from under her helmet and lashing them against her face. And the trees, the trees that had seemed so welcoming in the sunlight, now loomed black and craggy above their heads.

133

Libby followed Adam onto a dirt path that branched off the road into the woods, and soon up ahead in the murky shadows, she saw it: Raven Pond.

Her breath caught in her throat, and she had to grip the handlebars of her bike fiercely to stay steady. She knew this place. She'd been here before. In her dream.

A frothy fog sat heavy over the black water and whipped into peaks along the soggy banks, making it impossible to tell how big the pond actually was. Reeds and waterlogged brush stooped over the banks and spilled into the pond in places, collecting thick coats of algae.

Adam propped his bike up against a grizzled tree and surveyed the pond, shaking his head. "I forgot how much it looks like the setting for a horror film. Why would anyone ever come here for a picnic?"

"Julia and Kara were here in the spring," Libby said. "I'm sure it looked much prettier with all the trees budding." But to be honest, nothing around the pond looked like it was alive enough to bloom. Everything about the place was unsettling, and somehow, a little bit sinister.

"Well, I better get ready," she said, pulling off her jacket, and then her clothes. The pink flowered bathing suit she'd worn underneath was totally wrong for the temp, but she hadn't had a choice. It was the only suit she owned. "It looks like there's a storm coming." No sooner had the words left her mouth than needles of sleet began falling, painfully pricking her exposed skin and piercing the pond water.

Libby shivered, and Adam tossed her the wet suit.

"You're already freezing," he said, "and you're not even in the water yet." He frowned. "This was a bad idea. We shouldn't have come."

Libby zipped up the wet suit and tried to keep her teeth from visibly chattering. "This helps," she said, and it did. It just didn't help *that* much, but she wasn't about to let on how cold she really was. "Thanks." She stepped over to the edge of the bank, but as she did Adam put his hand on her arm.

"Libby, wait." His eyes held hers, his brow creased in worry. "This is serious stuff . . . dangerous even. You don't have to do this."

Libby hesitated, staring at the inky water. She was not a risk-taker or a daredevil. She had always lived out her adventures through the pages of her latest book, or followed Nina reluctantly into some new activity she wasn't really enthused about. Now, she was scared, same as always. Terrified, actually.

But there was no Nina to drag her into this, no one to pressure her, or pave the way for her, no book to tell her how it would turn out. It was just her . . . Libby. And she had to make this decision alone.

"Yes," she said firmly. "I *do* have to do this." And without glancing back at Adam again, without giving herself another minute for second-guessing, she walked into the water.

She gasped, her feet barely having time to feel the sludgy texture of the bottom before going completely numb. The water sucked her feet into its cavernous darkness, and she couldn't see them at all, even though she was only up to her ankles. She was going to be swimming blindly. How would she find anything? She glanced up at the sky, which was dimming with every passing second and sending wave after wave of sleet in earnest now. She was wasting time. Time she didn't have.

She took a deep breath and plunged forward, scrabbling past grasses that slithered across her calves and forearms, and propelled herself farther out toward the middle of the pond. Then she dived under and opened her eyes and saw nothing but endless black. She broke through the surface, took a quick breath, and dived again, this time trying to swim downward.

Come on, Julia, she begged silently with the nothingness surrounding her. *Show me what to do. Help me if you can.*

Then, in front of her, a murky face slowly took shape. Julia's face, eyes open and pleading.

Libby swam toward her face, pushing deeper into the darkness. Her ears throbbed with pressure, her nose ached, and she knew she was at least ten or twelve feet under. Julia's face was fading now, growing shadowy and faint.

Wait! was Libby's silent cry.

Then Julia's voice was inside her head, urgently whispering, *I can't stay here. Hurry.*

Libby stretched her hands toward the face, wanting to grab hold of it, make it stay with her. But it disappeared, just as Libby's fingers sunk into the oily bottom of the pond. Her lungs starting to burn, she spread out her fingers, sweeping them through layers of frigid muck until — there! — her fingers closed around something hard and metallic. This had to be it. She clutched it in her hand and pushed off the bottom with her feet, immediately shooting upward. But a sudden jerk on her right ankle wrenched her body back down. She shook her ankle frantically, feeling the grip of something tightening its hold on her. Reaching down, her fingers grazed against something slick and taut, wound impossibly tight. Her lungs were on fire now. She clawed at it, but she couldn't break free.

She fought the urge to inhale, knowing that she had only seconds left before her mouth would open against her will, seeking air and finding nothing but frozen water. She flailed, yanking her ankle, twisting away, reaching for the surface. But she was trapped, and she was running out of breath . . .

A faint beam of light shot through the water, inches from her face. Sunlight? Suddenly, Libby could see the band of grasses wrapped around her ankle. Feeling her last bit of strength leaving her, she reached down one last time, slipping the grasses over the heel of her foot. Her legs didn't want to cooperate, but she gave one last lunge toward the surface, and this time, her head broke through.

Coughing and gulping air all at once, she barely registered Adam's arms around her, pulling her toward the bank.

"Are you okay?" Adam sputtered between gasps. "You just disappeared in there. And the water went completely still. You really freaked me out."

"I'm okay," Libby stammered through chattering teeth when she was finally able to talk.

"You didn't tell me I'd be going for a swim, too," Adam said, motioning to his soaked jeans and sweater.

"Sorry." Libby brushed freezing drops of water from her face and hair. Her fingers would not stop quivering as Adam handed her a towel.

Libby gratefully took it as a fresh fit of coughing shook her. She wasn't sure she would ever feel warm again.

Adam clambered over to his backpack, pulling out another towel and an extra change of clothes. "Good thing I prepare for every possibility."

"My ankle got caught," Libby said. "I couldn't get it loose. I — I almost . . ."

"Don't think about it," he interrupted, sitting down next to her. "You're safe now." He piled his towel on top of the one Libby already had around her shoulders. "I think I saw a bathroom down the road a bit. We can take turns changing."

"Okay," Libby said, cocooning herself in the towels. "But aren't you going to ask me first?"

"I'm afraid to," he said quietly.

She smiled and slowly opened her trembling fist to reveal a chain of tarnished, algae-tinged roses. "I got it," she whispered. "I found Kara's bracelet."

Libby rubbed her hand across the steam-coated bathroom mirror, then held the bracelet up to the light. She'd spent the last half hour scrubbing it with an old toothbrush and her mom's jewelry cleaner. It wasn't sparkling with shine anymore, the way it probably had when Kara had worn it. But at least it was clean, free of the green muck and most of the rust that had encased it earlier.

She slid it carefully into the pocket of her jeans, then finished combing her freshly washed hair. She and Adam had said quick good-byes at the library, because it was already nearing two in the afternoon, and her mom had sent her a few not-so-subtle texts asking if she was okay, and how the studying was going. Adam may have been her tutor, but he was still a boy, so her mom felt compelled to check up on her.

"Well, let me know how the test goes tomorrow," Adam had said, and even with his hands shoved into his jacket pockets, Libby could see he was still shivering, too. "I'd wish you luck, but you don't need it. You've got the material nailed. You've got an A in the bag."

"Ha," Libby had said. "Don't be so sure."

"With a tutor like me?" Adam had grinned. "I wouldn't let you get away with anything else. As long as you remember your Austen characters, you'll remember the periodic table. Trust me." He'd hopped onto his bike. "Now if you'll excuse me, I have to get home before my fingers and toes fall off."

Libby had laughed. "Hey, Adam!" She'd caught up with his bike. "Thank you," she'd said, blushing. "For coming with me today, and for, well, you know, swimming in after me."

"No problem." Adam had smiled and shrugged, but — did she imagine it, or did his cheeks blaze a brighter red? "You just tell Julia that the next time an arctic swim is on the agenda, she needs to find somebody else to haunt."

Libby had laughed and watched him ride away, then she'd gone home to a deliciously hot bubble bath. And now, warmed and refreshed, with the clean bracelet tucked safely in her pocket, Libby was ready to take on her second, and hopefully last, challenge for the day. But this one, she'd have to do without Adam's help.

She walked over to the Griffins', knocked on the door, and waited. A soft shuffling came from the other side of the door, and then a drawn-out silence. She pictured Mrs. Griffin pressed against the door, holding her breath, debating whether or not to open it.

Please open it, Libby silently pleaded. *Give me one more chance.*

Finally, the door inched open and Mrs. Griffin's hesitant, solemn face peered around it. And then a barely audible, "Hello, Olivia."

"Hello, Mrs. Griffin," Libby said, trying to sound much more confident than she felt. "I know you've asked me not to come over. I'm sorry to disrupt your day, and I promise I'm not here to cause any trouble." She paused to take a breath, and Mrs. Griffin did not shut the door in her face. "I actually have something for Julia," Libby pressed on, the words coming quicker. "I'd like to give it to her myself, if you'll let me. It's something very important."

"Really?" Mrs. Griffin raised skeptical eyebrows. "What is it? I'm sure I can pass it on to her —"

"No," Libby said too loudly. Then a second time, quietly, "No. Please. Please believe that I wouldn't ask you for something like this unless I was sure . . ." She took a deep breath. "Unless I was certain that it needed to come from me. I wish I could explain more. But I really can't." She kept eye contact with Mrs. Griffin, refusing to waiver. "You can come with me, if you want. It will only take a minute. Please."

Libby stood motionless as Mrs. Griffin considered, afraid the slightest movement would destroy any chance she had. Then Mrs. Griffin sighed and swung the door wide.

"You get one minute," Mrs. Griffin said sternly as she led the way upstairs.

"Thank you," Libby said.

Mrs. Griffin waited by Julia's bedroom door as Libby stepped into the room. Julia had on different clothes today, but she still wore the same glazed expression as she sat unmoving in her bed. The room was like an impenetrable time capsule that nothing could alter. Well, that was about to change.

Libby leaned over Julia and slowly reached for her marble-like hand where it lay on top of the comforter. She nestled Kara's bracelet into Julia's palm, then gently closed her fingers over it.

"Here it is, Julia," she whispered. "Come see for yourself."

She smiled at Julia, hoping the girl's lifeless fingers could somehow sense the tiny roses resting within them. Maybe it would give Julia some peace. Maybe, just maybe, it would help her come back from wherever she was. It seemed impossible that something so small could have any effect on Julia at all. But with everything that had happened over the last few days, Libby was starting to become a big believer in the impossible.

She gave Julia's hand a squeeze of encouragement, quickly thanked a perplexed Mrs. Griffin, and went back home. She still had hours of studying to do for her test tomorrow, but she didn't care. A thrilling lightness flitted through her, and she smiled even as she settled onto her bed with the textbook she was so sick of looking at. She had done the right thing; she could feel it. She'd done everything she could for Julia, and the shadow that had weighed on her since she'd met Julia had lifted.

She studied until she couldn't keep her eyes open, and when she drifted off, it was into a serene and dreamless sleep.

CHAPTER TEN

Libby put down her pencil and rechecked her answers one last time. No, there wasn't a single one she would change. She was positive. She sat back in her chair, stretched her back in relief, and raised her hand.

Mrs. Kilchek tiptoed toward her. "Yes, Libby?" she whispered.

"You said to raise a hand when we were finished with the test," Libby said, relishing this moment.

"Yes, I did," Mrs. Kilchek said haltingly.

Libby held up her test. "I'm finished."

Mrs. Kilchek's eyebrows launched upward in surprise, then she leaned closer to Libby. "Are you sure? You still have five more minutes left to work."

"I'm sure, thank you." It was probably too early to risk a smile, but now one itched at the corners of Libby's mouth.

Mrs. Kilchek nodded, and Libby watched as her test moved away down the aisle, now at the mercy of Mrs. Kilchek. Well, that was that.

The five minutes flew, and when the bell rang Libby was already halfway out of her desk, scooting past most of her classmates, who were still frantically scribbling away at their tests. Her smile broke free and grew the second Libby stepped into the hallway.

She grabbed her cell phone out of her bag and quickly texted Adam. He would be finishing up his AP chem at Whitford High right about now.

Libby: Hey Einstein. U have a new rival. Guess who? ☺

Adam: I knew u would ace it! Congrats! PS. Don't get 2 cocky.

Libby: LOL

Adam: Want to hear the details. Call me l8tr?

Libby: K

Libby put her phone away, still beaming, but her smile collapsed when she glanced up to see Nina and Alia a few feet away. A small congregation of girls was gathered around Alia's locker, and Alia was waving Nina's cell phone in front of their faces to their appreciative "oohs" and "aahs." Nina stood next to her, smiling politely, blushing prettily, and looking just the slightest bit uneasy.

"Isn't it fab?" Alia said. She gazed at the photo glowing on the cell-phone screen again for reaffirmation, then passed it around for everyone to ogle again. "Nina wanted to go with a simple black dress with cap sleeves. But cap sleeves are so preschool. So I told her, 'no way.' It had to be this strapless flame-red mini instead."

"It's gorgeous," chimed in Selene, right on cue.

"It is really pretty," Nina said in a wavering, uncertain tone Libby had never heard from Nina before. Nina was usually bubbling over with self-confidence. Or at least, the old Nina was.

"See!" Alia nudged Nina in the side. "Aren't you glad I made you get it, Nina-bean?"

Libby cringed inwardly. *Nina-bean?* What, was Nina two now? How could she stand to be crooned at like that? It was awful.

But Nina just ducked her head and mumbled, "Um, yeah, Alia. You have great taste."

"I know!" Alia squealed, and all the other girls nodded and echoed praise in agreement.

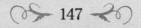

"So, can I have my phone back now?" Nina asked.

Alia waved her hand in the air, batting away the question. "In a minute," she said, her attention focused again on the cell. "I just want to show them the killer shoes we got for you."

Nina nodded, a tolerant smile pasted on her face. But Libby, who knew all of her facial expressions, could read Nina's irritation in the tightness of that well-practiced smile. Still, if Nina was annoyed, why was she putting up with this? Alia was so disgustingly condescending, and Nina had always had great fashion sense. She didn't need Alia telling her what to wear.

Suddenly, Nina glanced up and her eyes connected with Libby's. But she looked away immediately, hiding her face behind her hair.

Anger flared in Libby's stomach, and she wanted to turn away. But still, she hesitated, a new thought hitting her. Was it really that Nina didn't want to see Libby, or that Nina was so embarrassed she didn't want Libby to see *her*? This new Nina seemed to be trying so hard to please her newfound friends, but maybe that was because Nina didn't have another friend to turn to right now.

Libby took a step toward Nina. Maybe if she walked over, if she started with a simple "hi," then Nina would take it from there. But . . . no. Libby shook her head and turned away. This was the way Nina wanted it. It had to be. She hadn't given any sign of wanting to reconnect with Libby. And Libby couldn't forget how dismissive and distracted Nina had been with her over the past few weeks. No, no matter how much Libby missed their friendship, Nina was where she belonged.

Libby headed for the cafeteria, shaking off the frustration she felt about Nina and vowing to resume her cheery attitude. She wasn't going to let anything dampen her spirits today. She was going to finish the school day, and then go home to bake brownies to celebrate her science victory. Even if she didn't have Nina to share them with, they would still be delish.

As it turned out, she never had the chance to bake the brownies. Because when she stepped off the school bus, the first thing she saw was a barely recognizable Mrs. Griffin running — actually, physically *running* — right for her. And she was smiling — a brilliant, joyous Cheshire-cat grin that wiped the signature sadness off her face. *What is wrong with her?* Libby almost took a step back onto the bus, deciding she didn't want to know. But the bus pulled away too soon, leaving her on the curb to face whatever was coming alone.

"Libby!" Mrs. Griffin gushed breathlessly, taking her by the arm and enthusiastically pulling her up the driveway. "I'm so glad you're home. I've been waiting for your bus for ten minutes. The most amazing thing has happened." She laughed, shaking her head at the sky. "It's Julia! She's started talking again!"

Libby stopped and stared. "What?"

Mrs. Griffin nodded, her eyes gleaming. "She woke up this morning and . . . and it was like she just came back to herself."

"But . . . how?" A tentative smile was inching onto Libby's face.

"I don't know," Mrs. Griffin said. "It's a miracle. The doctors say these things can happen suddenly. They don't have an explanation, but . . ." She grinned. "Who cares? She's back, and that's all that matters."

"That's amazing," Libby said, her smile growing. "I'm so happy for all of you." And she meant it. After all the times she'd seen Julia over the past two weeks, now Julia would be a moving, talking person again. Alive in every sense of the word. It was incredible.

"Libby, it's the oddest thing." Mrs. Griffin placed both her hands on Libby's shoulders. "For some reason, Julia's been asking to speak with you."

Libby gulped. *That* she hadn't expected at all. "She has?"

"I don't even know how she knows who you are, but well, she does. Your name was the first thing she said when she woke up." Mrs. Griffin blushed and looked at the ground. "I know you and I had some misunderstandings, but I'd like to forget about all of that, if you're willing." Her eyes were pleading. "For Julia's sake, do you think you could come over and see her? Right now?"

"Of course," Libby said. And at that moment, there was nothing she wanted to do more.

Mrs. Griffin hurried her into the house and up the stairs, all the excitement of the day glowing on her skin, transforming her face into a younger, prettier one. It was wonderful to watch. But even more wonderful was when Libby stepped into Julia's room. Julia was standing on unsteady legs at the foot of her bed, her face a healthy pink, her eyes sparkling with life and happiness, her black hair shining. Half a dozen doctors and nurses surrounded her (including the mysterious lady doctor Libby had seen before). They were checking her vitals and reflexes and helping her take a few halting steps.

But then she glanced up, her eyes met Libby's, and a flash of recognition lit up her face. A broad smile broke over her cheeks, making her even more radiant.

"Hello, Libby," she said easily, as if they'd known each other for years.

"Julia." Libby grinned. "It's so nice to finally meet you in person."

CHAPTER ELEVEN

It took the doctors and nurses another fifteen minutes to finish their examination of Julia. They fluttered around her, taking notes and murmuring to one another about physical therapy and muscle atrophy. But overall, they seemed pleased with Julia's condition. Libby hadn't been completely sure whether she should stay or not. When she'd made a move to leave the room, though, Julia had stopped her. So Libby waited patiently, taking a seat in the armchair at the foot of Julia's bed.

But Julia, as it turned out, was not the greatest of patients. After the first five minutes, she was already waving away the blood-pressure cuff and stethoscope, saying, "Can't we finish with all the medical theatrics, please?"

"Absolutely not," Mrs. Griffin said, clearly horrified by the idea.

Julia rolled her eyes at Libby, then hung her head in exaggerated defeat. Libby grinned. She liked this new Julia already.

When the medical team finally said good-bye to Julia and stepped into the hallway with Mrs. Griffin to give their assessment, they clicked the door closed behind them. And, just like that, Libby and Julia were alone.

Libby met Julia's eyes, and smiled. "How do you feel?"

Julia shrugged. "Like I've been asleep for a year." She stretched her legs, wiggling her feet experimentally. "My body feels like a vat of Jell-O."

"I'm sure your doctors are going to give you exercises to help with that," Libby said.

"Good, because the sooner I can walk myself out of this bedroom, the better." Julia plucked at her comforter, her mouth crinkled in frustration. "This room feels like a crypt. And it smells like a hospital. I'm suffocating in here. I can't wait to go outside."

"I know exactly how you feel," said Libby, thinking of the restlessness she was feeling after being housebound for fourteen days. "Maybe your mom will let you come out for a little while later. It's cold outside today, but it feels good in the sun." Libby paused, taking a deep breath to prep for what she said next. "Julia, your mom said you were asking for me before. You even knew my name." She met Julia's eyes. "Do you know me?"

"I . . . I think so," she said quietly. Then she seemed to rethink and nodded firmly. "No, I know I do. I'm sure of it. It's the strangest thing. I remember all of these bizarre dreams. In some of them, I'm outside in the yard, or standing at my window looking out. I even had one where I was underwater." She shook her head, looking like she was trying to jiggle some confusing thought into its right place. "They're all a bit hazy. But when I try to remember, there's one thing I can see completely clearly." Her eyes were studying Libby's face intensely. "You. You were in every one of my dreams."

She reached for something on her nightstand. "When I woke up this morning, I was holding this." She opened her hand to reveal Kara's bracelet. "And somehow, I was sure you'd put it there. I don't know how that's possible. But your name was stuck in my head. And when I held the bracelet, I kept seeing your face."

Libby nodded at Julia, whose face was full of unanswered questions. "I think I can tell you why," she said, her heart galloping.

And slowly, Libby retraced the events of the last two weeks, starting with the first time she saw Julia in the front yard. Julia's eyes widened as she listened, and when Libby told her about the swim in Raven Pond, Julia visibly shuddered, her face paling.

"Are you all right?" Libby asked. She offered Julia the water glass off the nightstand. "I'm sorry. I probably told you too much. It's a lot to process."

"No," Julia said quietly after sipping the water. "Everything you described is exactly like I remembered from my dreams. Only . . ." She glanced out the window. "They weren't really dreams, were they? It was all real."

"Yes," Libby said. "I think a part of you came looking for someone who might be able to help you."

"Thank you for this." Julia ran a finger along the length of Kara's bracelet, tracing the outlines of the roses. "I needed this back so badly."

"Can I ask you something?" Libby said. "Why is the bracelet so important?"

Julia stared at it for a long time, her eyes welling with tears. Then she blew out a long, tired sigh. "It's a long story." She wiped her eyes. "That day at the pond, Kara and I weren't even supposed to swim. We had on winter coats and gloves. That's how cold it was outside. We'd just finished eating, and things were going okay. Except that Kara couldn't stop talking about Heather. The whole time." Her face sagged a bit. "I was so sick of hearing about Heather, and she wouldn't stop. And then . . ." She paused, and she seemed to be fighting an internal battle over her next words. "Then she told me that Heather had invited her to go to Florida over spring break."

"And that made you angrier," Libby said. She could imagine how she'd feel if Nina went someplace like that with Alia. She might have felt hurt and angry, too. But she would definitely have felt left out, at the very least.

"I'd already made plans with Kara for spring break," Julia continued. "We had talked about going to the movies, and going shopping." Her shoulders drooped. "I probably should have been more understanding. But Kara was just so laid back about it all. She said we could go to the movies anytime, but she could only go to Florida with Heather once."

"That must have been hard," Libby said.

"I acted like we had these unbreakable plans,"

Julia said. "But I was really just hurt I wasn't included in *her* plans." She took a deep breath. "And that's when I sort of . . . lost it."

"What do you mean?" Libby gripped the edge of her chair. She wasn't sure she wanted to hear what came next. What had Julia done?

"I screamed at her," Julia said in a hushed, breaking tone. "I told her we weren't friends anymore. That all she cared about was herself and that dumb bracelet Heather gave her. And then I ripped the bracelet off her wrist and threw it in the pond."

"Oh no," Libby whispered, guessing where this was probably heading.

Julia's eyes glistened. "Kara jumped right in after it. She made it to the middle of the pond and started diving under to find it. But then . . ." Julia closed her eyes, a tear rolling down one cheek. "Something went wrong. She started panicking in the water, screaming and coughing and going under. So I swam out to get her."

"That water must have been freezing," Libby said, remembering how cold it was when she'd been in it.

"It was, but I didn't care. I just wanted to help Kara. But when I got to her, she was crazy scared. I tried to help her, but she pulled me under. She wrapped her arms so tight around my neck, I couldn't stay above the surface. I couldn't even breathe."

"I'm sure she didn't know what she was doing," Libby said.

"I pulled her arms off," Julia said. "I had to, just to breathe. I was so tired by then. I reached for her again though." Tears coursed steadily down her cheeks now. "But . . . but she was already under."

"I'm so sorry," Libby whispered, putting her arm around Julia.

"She went in to get her bracelet," Julia said, "and it was all my fault."

"Everyone gets angry sometimes," Libby said, thinking of the grudge she'd been carrying against Nina the last few days.

"I should never have let it get in the way of our friendship," Julia said. "I was trying to force Kara to choose between Heather and me." She stared at her lap. "It wasn't fair of me."

"You had a right to be upset. You couldn't have known what would happen." But even as she said it, guilt struck a painful jab at Libby's heart. Choosing between friends. Wasn't that kind of what Libby was expecting from Nina, too? Libby hadn't ever even made an attempt to warm up to Alia or any of Nina's other new friends. She'd been too busy feeling sorry for herself, and too focused on staying angry with Nina.

Libby squeezed Julia's hand. "What happened to Kara wasn't your fault. It was just a horrible accident. You tried to help her. You did everything you could."

The two of them sat quietly for a few minutes. Libby could see the pain on Julia's face, and knew it would probably be a very long time before that would go away. It would be horrible to carry that guilt around all the time, which maybe explained what had happened to Julia after the accident. Maybe Julia's mind and body went into a holding pattern, just to give her the time she needed to cope.

It was Julia who finally broke the silence. "I haven't done *everything* I could . . . not yet." She held up the bracelet. "I have to give this back to Kara's family. She loved this bracelet so much. And maybe, in some way, it will make her family feel better to know that it's been found."

"I'm sure it will," Libby said. "And I'm sure Kara would be happy to know it's been found, wherever she is. You'll feel better afterward, too. Then you can work on getting your strength back."

"I hope you're right," Julia said with a small, sad smile.

Libby squeezed her hand, and just then, there was a light knock at the bedroom door, and Mrs. Griffin peeked in. "Are you two all right?" she asked. Then her eyes settled on Julia's tear-streaked face, and she was next to her on the bed in an instant. "What's wrong, sweetie? Have you been crying?"

Julia hugged her mom. "I'll be fine. I just need you to take me to the Johansens' when I feel a little better."

"Of course." Mrs. Griffin kissed Julia's forehead. "Of course I will."

"You know, I actually have somewhere I have to go, too." Libby stood up, giving them both a smile. "Julia, I'm so glad we got to talk. And maybe I'll see you at school soon?"

"I hope so," Julia said. "And Libby." She smiled. "Thanks . . . for everything."

"You're welcome," Libby said, and she quietly left as Julia started to explain to her mom about Kara's bracelet. Libby stepped out into the golden afternoon light and inhaled the crisp air, happiness warming her from the inside out. She *had* helped Julia, and she felt amazing just knowing that.

But Julia had helped her today, too. Julia had let jealousy destroy her friendship with Kara, and now, Libby was letting the same thing happen to her friendship with Nina. And Libby had made up her mind to do something about that, right now.

CHAPTER TWELVE

Libby rang the doorbell and held her breath. She wasn't sure how Nina would feel about seeing her, and she didn't have much time to find out. She'd left a note for her mom before she'd biked over to Nina's house, and had broken the rules by leaving, though she was hoping her mom would understand. And she needed to get home before dark so her mom wouldn't worry. Finally, the door slowly opened on a blushing and hesitant Nina.

"H-hey," Nina stammered awkwardly, then motioned to the strapless cherry mini that she had on. "I was just . . . just trying this on again." She hugged her bare shoulders, and Libby wasn't sure if she was protecting herself from the chilly breeze or if she was embarrassed. "I didn't know you were coming over."

"I didn't either," Libby said. "It was sort of spontaneous. We haven't talked lately and I . . . well, I missed you." She pushed through the awkward pause that followed. At least Nina hadn't slammed the door in her face yet. That was a promising sign. "I really like the dress," she tried. "Alia was right. Red looks so pretty on you." She was being sincere, too. The red in Nina's dress brought out the natural strawberry highlights in her hair, and made her green eyes pop. She looked great.

"Thanks," Nina said. "I do love the dress. I just wish it didn't show quite so much . . . skin." She giggled nervously and her cheeks blazed. "My mom told me I have to wear this over it, or I can't go to the Harvest Festival." She held up a plaid flannel shoulder wrap in tacky holiday reds and greens.

"Oh no." Libby shook her head.

"I know." Nina groaned. "It's awful."

"What else do you have in your closet?" Libby asked. Then it was her turn to blush awkwardly. "Maybe I could come in and help you look for something else?" She stared at the ground. "But only if you want me to," she added quickly.

But much to her relief, Nina didn't even hesitate.

"Yes," she said. "Yes, *please*. I could use all the help I can get."

Once they were in Nina's bedroom, Libby was grateful to have the clothes in the closet to focus on. It gave them both something to talk about that kept the awkwardness from taking over. It was still there, but they skirted around its corners, which was fine by Libby.

Libby pulled out half a dozen sweaters and wraps, but none of them did the trick.

"It's hopeless," Nina said, throwing herself on the bed. "I got all those clothes in Italy, and none of them work with this dress."

"We can't give up," Libby said. Then she remembered. "Hey," she said, plunking down on the bed next to Nina. "Would your mom settle for a black shrug? I have that black lace one you can borrow."

"If it gets me out of wearing a plaid grandma shawl, I'll wear anything," Nina said with a little laugh. "And I'm sure my mom will be okay with it."

"Oh, but wait . . ." Libby paused, remembering Alia's words. "It does have preschool cap sleeves."

Nina contemplated this, then shrugged. "*I* don't think cap sleeves are preschool. I think they're chic."

Nina looked sharply at Libby, and Libby knew Nina was remembering Alia's comment, too. "Alia is my friend," she said slowly, "but I don't have to agree with her all the time."

"Okay," Libby said with a small smile. She had to be careful here, because she didn't want to misstep with the wrong words. "You know, I feel like maybe I haven't been giving Alia a fair chance. I know you like hanging out with her. And I haven't really been okay with that."

"No," Nina said cautiously, "you haven't been." She fidgeted with the skirt of her dress. "But I've been pretty out of it lately, too. I know you've been stuck in your house studying for two weeks straight, and I never once asked you how it was going. I should've paid closer attention."

"Well, I wasn't in the greatest of moods, anyway," Libby said. "I was actually a little jealous."

Nina popped out a surprised laugh. "Jealous? Of what?"

"Of you," Libby said, sighing. "You've been different since you got back from Italy. Alia and her friends think you're cool and interesting. You didn't really seem to want to be around me much anymore. And, well . . ." Okay, it was time for the big confession. She braced herself, leaning on the mattress for support. "I was mad because Zack liked you, instead ... instead of me." She sucked in a breath as her cheeks burned. There. She'd finally said it.

A full ten seconds went by before Libby chanced a glance at Nina's face. Nina was staring at Libby, mouth open in an astonished O.

"You're serious," Nina whispered. "*You* have a crush on Zack?"

"*Had*," Libby said. "I had a crush ... since third grade."

Nina threw herself backward onto the bed, sunk her face into a pillow, and screamed. "You had a crush on Zack for the last four years and you *never* told me? Libby?!" She gave Libby a little shove to the shoulder. "How could you?"

Libby held up her hands in mock self-defense. "I never told anyone. I always knew it would never happen, so I figured it was pointless to even talk about it."

Nina rolled her eyes. "You should have told me, Lib," she said, horrified. "I would never have agreed to go to the dance with him if I'd known. I would never have even talked to him in the first place!" She shook her head.

"It's okay," Libby said. "I'm not even mad about it anymore." And as soon as she said it, she realized it was true. Ever since he'd asked her about Nina's favorite flowers, Zack Northam had dropped out of Libby's mind. Now she remembered, with a little annoyance, his comments about the Harvest Festival theme. She'd always known Zack didn't have much in common with her, but maybe she'd just never realized how much that could matter until now. She looked Nina square in the eyes, and took a deep breath. "Look," she said, "if Zack likes you and you like him, you should go to the festival together. You shouldn't miss out on that just because I got some silly crush when I was eight."

"Really?" Nina asked doubtfully.

"Really." Libby smiled to let her know that it was all fine.

"Good," Nina said, sighing with relief. "But I'm still sorry I didn't know sooner. And I'm sorry for the way I've been acting lately, too. I think I've maybe been a tiny bit distracted?"

Libby laughed, and pinched her fingers together to illustrate. "Maybe just a *tiny* bit. All of a sudden, it was Aliapalooza around you."

Nina ducked her head apologetically. "I know. I

was just so happy to have Alia inviting me to hang out. I missed spending time with you, and Alia was around when you weren't. And then I got mad at you because you seemed irritated that I was spending time with her. I didn't think it was fair for you to expect me to sit home by myself just because you couldn't go anywhere."

"It wasn't fair of me to expect that," Libby said. "I was wrong."

"But I was, too," Nina said. "I should've thought more about how it might make you feel, especially when you were under virtual house arrest."

"Yeah, it was bad timing," Libby said, "but I could've tried harder. I could've told you sooner about Zack, and that I felt a little left out when Alia came into the picture. So, I'm sorry, too."

"You know, Alia is a lot of fun." Nina smiled. "But I'm always going to need my BFF time with you. You've known me my whole life. You know everything about me. And Alia . . ." She glanced down at her dress. "Well, she's not always the greatest listener, like you are. She can get a little wrapped up in herself sometimes."

"Well, when that happens, you come over to my house for brownies, right?"

"Always," Nina said, and the two of them hugged. "So, now that I've got my wardrobe crisis under control, what's been happening with you?"

Libby grinned, and took a deep breath, thinking of all the things she couldn't wait to tell her. Where would she start? And then she knew. Julia. It had all started with Julia. And finally, now that she knew Nina was listening, she would tell her every single detail. Because that's what best friends do.

Libby parked her bike in the garage just as the first stars blinked into the sky. She hurried through the garage door into the kitchen, bracing herself for an argument with her mom, or her dad, or both of them. Her mom hadn't called her cell, which was a good sign. But still, Libby knew she'd come home later than she was usually supposed to. And besides, she hadn't officially been released from her "no after-school activities" dictate, so technically her mom could have a legit case against her.

Her mom was at the stove with her back turned, and Libby had to fight the urge to flee straight to her room.

"Um, hi," she said, hurrying past her mom to make a break for the stairs. "I'm sorry I'm late."

She had one foot on the stairs when her mom called out, "Hey! Get back in here, missy!"

Libby sighed and dropped her head to the wall. "Here it comes," she whispered, and she trudged back into the kitchen.

Her mom had a spaghetti-sauce laden spoon poised in midair like a divining rod ready to unleash the wrath. "You've been gone quite a while, and I don't recall ever having said you were allowed to go anywhere."

"I know," Libby started. "I left you a note, and I can explain everything —"

Her mom waved the spoon. "Stop right there." She furrowed her eyebrows sternly. "You broke the rules. But, it just so happens I'm feeling very lenient today, so you're off the hook." Then, a huge smile broke across her face. She dropped the spoon in the pot on the stove and grabbed Libby in an enthusiastic hug. "Congratulations, honey. I'm so proud of you!"

"Um, thanks," Libby mumbled into her mom's shoulder, trying to make sense of her mom's sudden personality change. "For what?"

Her mom blinked at her, clearly waiting for understanding to dawn on Libby. When it didn't, she said, "Didn't Adam tell you?"

Libby was getting more and more confused by the second. "Adam?"

Her mom threw up her hands. "Oh for goodness' sake. Yes, *Adam*! He's sitting on the front steps, waiting for you. Didn't you see him when you came in?"

"No," Libby called over her shoulder, because she was already hurrying through the foyer to the front door, her heart racing. There was Adam, sitting on the front steps with a supersized Shake Shop cup next to him. He looked up when she skidded to a stop in front of him, and gave her a wide grin.

"Hi." He held up the cup to her. "Chocolate-chip cookie-dough shake, just for you."

"Thanks," Libby said, taking it and sitting down next to him on the steps. Why was she suddenly so nervous? "You came all the way over here to give me a shake?"

"Yeah." His grin widened. "But also to congratulate Olivia Mason, Whitford Middle School science genius."

"I highly doubt there's a science genius here," Libby said. "I told you I *thought* I did great on the test, but I haven't even gotten my grade back yet. It's a little early to celebrate."

"Hmmm." Adam nodded, a rebellious brown lock falling across his forehead. "But what if I told you I stopped by Mrs. Kilchek's room after school? And that she'd graded your paper already?"

Libby swallowed thickly, her stomach flip-flopping. "You're kidding," she managed to stammer.

"Nope." Adam shrugged. "She knows I've been tutoring you, so she didn't mind telling me your grade."

Libby waited while Adam leaned back on the steps, stretching out his legs and yawning with theatrical exaggeration. Clearly he was planning on prolonging her torture, so she slugged him on the arm. "Adam! *Tell me!*"

"Okay, okay!" Adam laughed. "You got an A."

"Yes!" Libby shrieked and threw her arms around Adam. Then, after one second of delirious joy, she froze. Was she actually hugging Adam? Right now? On her front porch? She jerked back and tucked her hands into her lap, heat lighting up her face.

"Sorry," she said in answer to Adam's surprised face. Oh, this was so completely embarrassing. "I just got a little excited."

Adam gave a little laugh. "That's all right. Really." He cleared his throat awkwardly, and looked up at the sky, his cheeks two ripe tomatoes. "Mrs. Kilchek was a little excited, too. But thank goodness there was no hugging involved."

Libby laughed, and they broke through the awkwardness. "I'm surprised she didn't think I cheated," she said.

"No," Adam said. "In fact, she thinks this is a big-time breakthrough. She's expecting nothing less than A's from now on."

Libby groaned. "I hope you're not planning on quitting tutoring anytime soon."

"No worries," he said. "Your parents put me on the payroll." They smiled at each other, and then Adam's cheeks reddened all over again.

"You know, there was another reason I stopped by," he said hesitantly. He'd begun rubbing his eyebrow, and Libby held her breath, sensing something big was coming. Adam took a deep breath, then blurted, "I wanted to see if you would go to the Harvest Festival with me."

Libby's pulse was a gong in her ears, already pounding out the answer before she had a chance to speak. It was the last thing she'd expected him to say, but the bubble of joy percolating inside her meant that a part of her was glad he had. Or maybe more than just a part of her? She thought back over the last couple of weeks. Adam had listened when she'd had no one else to talk to. He'd believed her when she told him stories about Julia that sounded crazy, even to her. And he'd gone with her to the pond. He'd helped her every step of the way. Not just with her science, but with everything. He was a great friend (even if he did spout Einstein gibberish every once in a while). And — she would finally allow herself to admit it — maybe he could turn into more than a friend someday. There was actually no one she would rather go to the festival with — even Zack.

She smiled at Adam now, even as he stared at the brick steps, burying his chin in the collar of his jacket shyly.

"Yes," she said. "I'd love to go to the Harvest Festival with you."

"You would?" Adam said, his eyes lighting up.

"Yup. On one condition." She held up a finger. "Absolutely no science jokes of any kind."

Adam smiled. "Darn. And I had a great one about beakers, too." He laughed. "Kidding!"

"Good." Libby took a sip of her shake, and her mind began racing with a list of things she had to do before the festival on Friday. Thursday after school she had to help Nina and the rest of the committee hang all of the finished decorations in the gym. But top priority right now was finding something to wear. Something modern, but with a little bit of gothic finesse. Maybe her mom would agree to take her to the mall tomorrow after school. She was sure her mom would let her go, now that she had a great test score under her belt. She'd have to call Nina ASAP to see if she could come. And, maybe Julia, too? Julia hadn't been to a mall in six months! Of course she had to invite Julia!

"Libby?" Adam's voice cut into her thoughts. "Earth to Libby?"

"Sorry," Libby said. "I was just thinking that I'd have to ask Nina and Julia to go shopping with me to find a dress."

Adam's eyes widened. "Julia? Since when can ghosts go shopping?"

Libby slapped a hand to her forehead. "Adam! I can't believe I haven't told you yet! Julia woke up! This morning!"

"Whoa," Adam said, shaking his head in disbelief. "It was Kara's bracelet. Part of her must have known you'd found it. That's what did it."

Libby laughed. "I don't know what did it, but here's what happened . . ."

As Libby began talking, a light snow flittered down from the sky, dusting the brown grass with white lace. Libby should have been cold, but she wasn't. All the excitement of the day thrummed through her, warming her. She'd seen Julia awake, alive, and happy; she'd aced her test; and Adam was taking her to the festival. And for this one moment, everything was absolutely perfect.

CHAPTER THIRTEEN

Libby looked up at the glistening red chandeliers hanging from the ceiling of the gym. Their light cast glowing red diamond patterns on the floor and walls, and bounced off the skeletons and bats draped in the corners. Ornate candelabras bordered the dance floor, and deep-seated, tattered armchairs were scattered around the outskirts of the gym for kids needing a break from dancing. Some kids were lined up to get their photos taken in the satin-lined caskets set up along the bleachers, others were at the game booths, and a handful were admiring the enormous spiderweb draped from floor to ceiling at the corner of the dance floor.

"I don't think you've stopped smiling since we

walked in," Adam said to her as they swayed to the music.

Libby's cheeks warmed. "I can't help it. I'm just so happy with the way everything turned out." She smiled at Adam, and he suddenly swooped her into a dramatic dip. She giggled as he righted her back to her feet.

"The *Northanger Abbey* theme was a great idea," Adam said. "The gym looks awesome. And so do you."

"Thank you," Libby said, beaming. She'd chosen a simple, vintage-style velvet dress, loving the rich amethyst hues of the fabric. But her favorite part of the whole outfit was the black lace choker she'd found at Old Things New Consignment with Nina. There was a single teardrop crystal dangling from the center, and when Libby put it on, she felt just like one of the heroines from her novels.

And Adam wasn't doing too badly playing the part of her dashing hero either. In his black pants and crisp silvery blue shirt that matched his eyes exactly, Adam looked especially cute. It turned out that he was a really good dancer, too. Much better than most of the other guys on the dance floor. Libby had even seen Zack accidentally tripping on Nina's toes more than once tonight. So maybe royal princes didn't have all the charm after all. Libby had talked with Zack more tonight than she ever had before. And the more she'd learned about him, the more she'd seen how little they actually had in common. When Zack had told her that he hated to read, Libby had practically winced with pain at the idea of all the wonderful books he was missing out on. That was another great thing about Adam. He loved to read. Sure, most of it was science fiction, but she was going to turn him into an Austen fan yet.

She would never, ever admit this to Nina, but it gave her the teensiest bit of guilty pleasure to see that Zack was not quite as perfect as Libby had always imagined. Then again, maybe he *was* perfect for Nina. Just not for her. And that was fine with Libby.

"*Ciao, bella*," Nina called out to her now as she spun by with Zack. "Break for some punch after this song?"

Libby nodded, exchanging wide grins with Nina. They were all having so much fun tonight. They'd started off with the haunted hayride through the school parking lot. Then they'd ridden the Ferris wheel and Tilt-A-Whirl before coming inside to the gym for the dance. Dee and Aubrey had gone on the rides with them, too, and now were taking turns dancing with each other and with a few good-natured guys who were being dragged against their will onto the dance floor.

When the slow song ended, Libby and Adam made their way over to the refreshments table. Nina was already there with Zack, and Alia, Selene, and Vera hovered around them, chatting.

Libby hesitated for just a second, thinking it might just be better to wait until Alia moved on. But Adam was already striding over, totally oblivious to any social faux pas he might be committing, so Libby had no choice but to follow him.

Libby stepped up to Nina, almost expecting Nina to blush with embarrassment. But Nina's eyes lit up when she saw Libby, and she grabbed her by the arm and tugged her and Adam into the circle.

Libby offered Alia and her girls a tentative wave. She wasn't expecting much in return, so she had to consciously keep her mouth from falling open when Alia gave her an enthusiastic smile.

"Hi, Libby!" Alia said brightly, as if conversations between the two of them were the norm. "We were just talking about you." She leaned toward her. "Nina told me that this whole gothic-glam theme was your idea." She gestured toward the decorations. "I love it. It makes me think of Thornfield Hall. You know, from *Jane Eyre*?" Her eyes lit up. "Have you read it?"

Libby stared. Okay, now there was no helping the gaping mouth. It was hanging out there, and Libby didn't even care. Alia, reigning queen of WMS, had read *Jane Eyre*? This was a revelation of massive proportion. "Um, yeah," Libby managed to stammer. "It's one of my favorites." Maybe there was hope for Alia yet.

There was a moment of stilted awkwardness when no one seemed to know what to say next. Finally, Alia ran her hands through her hair to smooth it and cleared her throat. "Well," she said, looking at Nina. "We'll see you guys on the dance floor. Have fun!"

Then she and Selene and Vera walked to some of the armchairs, tucked themselves glamorously into them, and began chatting with the other members of the WMS royal court. Libby watched them for a moment, wondering if the world had actually tilted on its axis. For a few brief seconds, the lines between cliques had vanished, and she had seen a side of Alia that was surprising, and even wonderful. Things had shifted back into place now, and everyone's respective social lives had managed to stay intact. And that was fine with Libby. She didn't mind being a middling, especially when she had friends like Nina and Adam beside her.

She didn't think things could get much better, but then the gym doors opened, and they did. Because standing in the doorway, the moonlight brightly silhouetting her against the night, was Julia. For just a second, Libby wavered. Was this the real Julia? If she walked over to her, would she vanish, like she had so many times before? But, no. Libby knew beyond any doubt now. All she had to do was look at Julia and she could tell. There was nothing ghoulish about her tonight. Her fern green dress set off her shining black hair and brought out the lovely apricot color of her cheeks. And even though her legs still looked a bit thin from lack of use, she was standing straight and tall. Her eyes were glittering and lively, and her smile was wide and welcoming. The sickly pallor and sadness that had marked her face before had vanished. This was the real Julia. This Julia was brimming with life.

Libby rushed over to her. "Julia, I'm so glad you came. I wasn't sure your parents would let you."

"My mom tried to stop me," Julia said. "But then I told her I was going to go catatonic on her if she didn't let me come." She giggled. "It worked. I figure I can maybe use that two or three more times before she realizes I can't actually make good on the threat."

Libby laughed. "How are you feeling?"

"Okay." Julia stuck out one foot and swiveled her ankle experimentally. "My legs and arms still feel a little wobbly, but the physical therapist says that will get better soon. And my parents said I could start classes on Monday."

"That's great!" Libby said.

"Yeah, it'll be nice to get out of my house," Julia said. "But not so nice to have to catch up on half a year's worth of homework."

"I'll help you get caught up," Libby said. "I'm good at every subject except science. But I do know a great science tutor."

"Perfect." Julia looked at the floor, and a small trace of the old sadness reappeared on her face. "You know," she said quietly, "I saw Kara's parents yesterday afternoon. They stopped by our house."

"Wow," Libby said. "How was it?"

"Sad, but in a way, also amazing." Julia smiled. "This whole time I was afraid they were so angry with me. But when I saw them, they just seemed so happy that I was okay again. They weren't mad at all."

"Did you give them the bracelet?" Libby asked.

Julia nodded. "It felt so good to give it to them. I feel lighter all of a sudden, like maybe Kara's happy with me for doing it."

"I'm sure she is," Libby said. Then she smiled at Julia. "I know you and Nina met the other day at the mall, but are you ready to meet my other friends?"

"I don't know," Julia said uncertainly. "Are they dead or alive?"

"Very funny," Libby said. "For your information, I don't make a habit of befriending the living dead. *You* were the exception."

"Just making sure," Julia teased.

Libby led her over to Nina, Adam, and Zack, who were all waiting with welcoming smiles.

"Everyone, I want to introduce you to the girl next door," Libby said.

And as the five of them started talking, Libby

looked at Julia and happiness coursed through her. The two of them had been through so much together already, but now, for the first time, they could really get to know each other. Because Julia wasn't just the girl next door anymore. She was a wonderful new friend — a friend with a true, strong spirit.

BITE INTO THE NEXT POISON APPLE, IF YOU DARE....

There was a knock at the door. "Is everything okay?" a voice asked. It was Sean.

I opened the door, wide enough so he could see inside. "What do you think?" I asked him.

Sean took one look at the room behind me. "Either you are completely crazy, or there's a ghost in the inn," he said. "I'm going to go with the ghost."

I felt so relieved I almost started crying.

He looked deadly serious. "I guess I know why you were asking me about ghosts the other day. I assumed you were making fun of me. But . . ."

"I wasn't. Weird things keep happening, and I'm getting all the blame. I just thought maybe you'd know something that might help me. Like if there really is a ghost haunting this place, and pulling these tricks, then maybe everyone wouldn't be so mad at me."

"I totally understand," he said. "And I am going to help you get to the bottom of this."

A feeling of relief and gratitude washed over me. I was a little terrified, too. "Why do you think the ghost is picking on me?" I asked. "Doing things so I'll get blamed for them? Sending me messages and tearing up my room like this?"

Sean took a deep breath. "I think she may be a restless spirit who identifies with you somehow. She obviously thinks you can help, right?"

"Help with what?" I asked.

"We have to figure that out," Sean explained. "Then maybe the ghost will be able to find peace and will leave you alone."

"You know a lot about ghosts," I said.

"After I thought I saw her that night, I read a lot of books on the subject," he said. "But I have to say, your experiences have been way more intense than mine."

"Lucky me," I muttered.